Mark Hayhurst was brought up in and lives in Yorkshire – realising its only widespread representation so far was four old men in a tin bath and a farm that a plane crashed into, he knew that a flipside was needed. He doesn't see the point in writing anything that doesn't provoke a response so don't be surprised to feel repulsed, shocked, offended and a little ashamed at yourself for what you end up finding funny.

Friday at
The Nobody Inn

MARK HAYHURST

PaperBooks

First published 2007 by PaperBooks
PaperBooks Ltd, Neville House, Station Approach
Wendens Ambo, Essex CB11 4LB
www.paperbooks.co.uk

ISBN 1-906231-00-1
ISBN 978-1-906231-00-2

Cover design by Chris Gooch – Bene Imprimatur Ltd

Typeset by SetSystems Ltd, Saffron Walden, Essex
Printed and bound in Great Britain by
Cox & Wyman, Reading

This book is for Catherine,
Debnam, Jen and Ziggy.

There are a few people I need to thank without whom this book wouldn't be anywhere near as good. So here's to all the parties, crazy conversations and life experiences that have influenced me: Justin, Craig, Paul, Marcus, Russ, Kaye Boy, Sarge, Sarah, Jono and Tiz – cheers!

se′cret *a.* kept, meant to be kept, from general knowledge; hidden; private. – *n.* thing kept secret. – **se′cretly** *adv.* – **se′crecy** *n.* keeping or being kept secret; ability to keep secrets.

FRIDAY 13th July

At least today it would all be over one way or another; they'd either be dead, in prison or completely in the clear. Whatever the outcome, they'd be out of the whole sticky mess they'd got themselves into once and for all.

CHAPTER ONE

FRIDAY 8th June - 8 a.m.

The room looked like a tab end and a third full glass bomb had just exploded in it and the liquid in those glasses was definitely a sign that this party had gone far beyond far too late and was now way too early. Gone were the civilised empty bottles of lager and the tidy, short, mixer and ice combinations that people had been drinking, smiles on their faces, hours before. The evidence definitely gave away the fact that this little party had gone on too long. The sickly, pungent aroma of sambuca, last Christmas' port and old cooking wine rolled around the room. Rather than escaping through the half open window, the breeze and wafting of the curtains seemed to be giving the stench momentum.

Bang in the middle of this mess was Martin, displaying the only expression possible of someone who had munched, snorted and smoked his way through more than what would be considered a fair share of the party prescription; a confused gurn. To look at the state of him lying there you wouldn't think that only eight hours earlier, he was belting out quality tune after quality tune to a packed student night. This morning, he just looked a bit simple. He was lying in the foetal position amongst all this crap, the dark stains on the carpet near him offering clear evidence that he'd been twitching and knocking glasses over in his state of semi-consciousness. Not that it mattered; it was his house after all.

The drummer, Steve, had just come to with a start. He could hear music and a rhythmic banging noise coming from the bedroom upstairs and he glanced around the room. Christ, the fucking racket. If Jimbob needed to knock one out he should just go to the loo and do it discreetly, rather than go upstairs and belt one off full force in Martin's bedroom, using music to cover up his tommy-tanking.

Steve stood, pausing for a moment as if using some kind of as yet undiscovered radar technology to plot a way through all the shite in the room and get to the hallway. Off he popped, perfectly dodging every bit of party shrapnel along the way. He exited the room into the hallway and stood for a brief second at the bottom of the steps before quietly ascending; it would be much more embarrassing for Jimbob to be caught in the act than simply told to shut up. He'd stop knocking one out then for sure.

Steve ascended slowly. The stairs formed a U-shape and as he got to the top of the first third of them, he turned around and glanced upward through the gaps in the upstairs banister, into Martin's bedroom. Jimbob wasn't wanking, however; he was getting fired into some young bird Steve vaguely remembered seeing a few hours earlier. The sly fucker, thought Steve; he waits until we've passed out and then gets stuck into some groupie.

'Be rude not to,' thought Steve and continued advancing towards the door.

From downstairs, Martin heard a scream and a couple of accompanying banging noises which nudged him out of his stupor. He sat up to see a young girl running down the stairs. She stopped in the doorway and shouted at him, 'Your mates are wankers!' before bolting out of the door.

Confused, but glancing at his watch, Martin realised that he had more important things to worry about. Like them all getting their heads straightened out for an important photoshoot in a few hours. He opened the curtain that was blowing from the open window and the brightness and reality of Holme Bridge village this early in the morning petrified him.

It was hardly surprising; tucked neatly away in its own

little corner of Yorkshire, it was quiet, unassuming, rural and most of all deceptive because nothing there was quite what it seemed.

At the heart of the village sat a pub, *The Nobody Inn*. The locals that frequented it harboured dark secrets, and unbeknown to each of them, over the six weeks following Friday the eighth of June, their lives would become intrinsically linked; their secrets would burst at the seams and their lives would follow a path of madness, mayhem, mania and a relentless descent into self-induced destruction.

It was early morning and already Shirley was busy cleaning and polishing the pub. She spent so much time looking after the presentation of the place that her own appearance had taken a back seat over the years; her once shiny blonde hair was limp and lifeless and she'd started to develop dark rings under her baby blue eyes from the lack of sleep. It wasn't all bad though; the one thing she was happy with as a result of her action-packed régime was the weight she'd lost. She used to struggle to get into a size twelve but could now fit comfortably into an eight. To look at her go you could see why, she meant business. She was wearing an apron designed by her husband that was like a cleaning equivalent to Batman's utility belt, only rather than housing grappling hooks and bat-shaped boomerangs it came equipped with cleaning products and dusters of various colours and sizes.

On hearing a thud coming from the roof above her, Shirley dropped her duster, her husband, Dave, must have broken his routine and got out of bed early. She immediately began to worry that she'd not have enough time to finish off all of her chores before the pub needed opening. Quick as a flash she dropped to her knees and swiped the duster before it blemished the polished wood surface, then sighed with relief and regained her composure. She needed to hit on a tactic to delay him. Then it came; make him a nice cup of tea, so that once out of the shower he'd rest for a few minutes and read the paper whilst he enjoyed it.

She walked behind the bar, through the door at the back, up the stairs and into the flat above then slipped stealthily past the steamed-up bathroom and entered the kitchen. It was pristine, almost clinically so, not a speck of dust or a smudge in sight. The combined smells of Mr Muscle, Flash and Cif hung in the air like a constant reminder that it didn't just look clean, it really was clean.

Shirley filled up the kettle and put it on to boil; she took out a large mug with the words, *World's Best Landlord* in thick black letters written round. Next, she took out a teabag, a measuring jug, a spoon, a knife, the sugar jar, a tea towel, a glass into which she poured a shot of whisky, a small polythene bag, a bottle of full-fat milk and a stop-watch. She carefully laid each of these items out in a neat line on the worktop in front of her.

Shirley poured steaming water into the measuring jug until it reached precisely three hundred millilitres then transferred it into the mug. She picked up the teabag, placed it in the cup, started the stop-watch and waited for exactly thirty-five seconds before removing it, putting it into the polythene bag, tying a knot in the top and throwing it into the bin, a perfect shot. She grabbed the tea towel and used it to dry the jug, then took the milk, filled it to the twenty millilitre mark then added it to the tea. She scooped out a heaped teaspoon from the sugar bowl but, to ensure the consistency of her sugar delivery, she carefully used the back of the knife to level off the mound until it was a perfect straight. She added this to the mug and put everything, except the glass of whisky, away. By this time Dave had taken a seat in the living room and picked up his copy of *Pub Speak*. Shirley stirred the tea seven times clockwise and then seven times anti-clockwise, before taking a deep breath to calm her nerves. She downed the whiskey, picked up the mug and took it through to the living-room.

Shirley placed the mug on top of a coaster and waited nervously to make sure everything met with his approval. Dave folded over his paper and placed it next to the tea, never once making eye contact with her. He reached into his pocket and removed a thermometer. Terrified, Shirley suddenly realised that she'd forgotten to check the temperature and began to silently pray that she'd managed to fluke it. Dave shook the thermometer and dipped it into the tea. To Shirley's surprise and delight it was perfect. She managed to conceal her joy as she walked slowly out of the flat and into the pub below to finish off the morning's preparation.

It's hard to understand how the boys could tell the difference between day and night and night and day, but they always managed to wake up in the morning. This was pretty difficult considering they were confined to one completely dark room with no visible source of light. This morning Bobby woke up first and challenged his brother Billy to a round of hide and seek. It was their favourite game.

'OK then Bobby, as long as I can count first,' Billy said

before he began to count to ten slowly. Bobby simply took one sidestep to the left. He was impressed with his tactic.

'Ready or not, here I come!' Billy shouted, and began to hop around in the pitch darkness waving his arm around. Bobby expertly ducked and dodged each wave silently. After a while, Billy stopped face to face with his brother. Bobby was unsure if he'd been spotted but his uncertainty was soon quashed as he heard his brother shouting, 'Come out, come out wherever you are!'

Dave had just begun his daily pub inspection. He insisted on and strived for perfection. He was the most immaculately presented and groomed landlord you'd ever be likely to see, from the slip-ons on his feet to the Dax on his shiny slicked back hair. He stood with the posture of a royal holding his clipboard in front of him. His pub was of the small Yorkshire village variety and was as beautiful and quaint as it was clean; an old building with wooden beams across the roof and two large open fires at either end. It comprised two sections, the tap room and the restaurant. His inspection began, as always, around the corner from the bar in the dining area, a small collection of six tables which each sat four people. Shirley had already been awarded a tick in each of the boxes on Dave's list for arranging them correctly; the flowers were dead centre and the cutlery was so polished you could see your reflection bounce straight back at you from each piece. He measured the distance of each of the chairs from the table and ticked another couple of boxes on his list. Perfect. Then he turned his attention to the fireplace at the back of the room. The fresh flowers at each side were set precisely two centimetres in, diagonally, on the hearth. Tick! Tick! He reached into his pocket and pulled out a pair of white gloves, carefully put them on, dragged his gloved index finger across the top of the fireplace and inspected the miniscule grains of almost invisible dust on his otherwise sheet white glove.

'Disgusting!' he boomed. Shirley tried to explain but was abruptly cut off.

'I don't need excuses, Shirley. I need action!' He reached into his other pocket, pulled out a duster and flung it full force at her face. It fell to the floor and as Dave marched around the corner to check the bar, Shirley bent over, picked it up and gave the top of the fireplace another wipe.

'Chop, chop, Shirley! Stop this dilly-dallying!' He stormed over to Shirley, grabbed her roughly by the arm and dragged her to the bar. Dave looked across and scrutinised the fridges she'd filled. They were immaculate. The glass shone brightly both inside and out and every one of the bottles was polished and buffed to perfection. All the labels were facing forward and she had even implemented his stringent stock rotation policy; the old ones to the front and the new ones to the back. Dave turned to look at Shirley and took a long, slow, deep breath before growling, 'You should be ashamed of yourself.' She looked confused, everything was perfect.

'You know on a Friday we only have four rows of Budweiser and an extra row of Smirnoff Ice.'

'It's just so much to remember, Dave,' she squeaked.

Dave shook his head, reached over the bar and put his hand under the other side. He removed a large lever arch ring binder full to bursting with the word *Friday* written along the spine.

'It's all in the book!' he shouted as he slammed it down on the bar.

'It's just so much to remember Dave, you keep changing the ru . . .'

'If we're to run a professional establishment we need standards. I didn't get where I am today by leaving dust on fireplaces and filling fridges willy-nilly with no care, consideration or attention paid to what the drinking public may or may not wish to purchase on any given day. The rules need to be changed regularly to keep us abreast of public demand. They are under constant review and all I ask is that you read the manuals and prepare accordingly. Jesus! We don't open until twelve noon; that gives you at least seven hours to complete these tasks. Do you want to see this place go down the pan? Is that what you want? Where would we be then? In a Brewery-run wine bar? Or a managed house? Look, look on the wall over there — what does that say?'

Dave pointed at a shining plaque on the back wall near the entrance. Shirley hung her head and mumbled, 'Landlord of the year nineteen-eighty-nine'. Dave grabbed her face and forced it upwards so she was staring right at him.

'That's right,' he said, 'I met you in nineteen-ninety and haven't won another fucking award since! I don't know why I waste my time!' He released his grip and marched off behind the bar towards the pub kitchen.

'I'm sorry, Dave! I'll try harder, I promise.'

'I don't want you to try, Shirley, I want you to do! Now, go and vacuum the car park whilst I buff my nails, we open in three hours!'

Just around the corner from *The Nobody Inn*, about a half mile down on the left hand side, sat S-Packers, the village's biggest employer. The building used to be a cotton mill many moons ago and still retained some of its old charm around the exterior. It was a massively wide, incredibly high picturesque stone structure, littered with small, old-world windows. It was one of the few buildings of its type around Yorkshire that had not been snapped up by property developers using government grants to turn them into 'Luxury Apartments'. Nowadays it simply provided product packaging solutions, nothing complicated, just simple donkeywork.

The donkey of the office area, Clive, was scurrying around delivering mail and making cups of tea. It suited him, all that scurrying; he was a weird looking little dweeb – you could picture him twenty years back as being one of those children with grubby clothes, dirty knees, hair that would probably be a sandy colour if you cleared out the grease and a small crusty trail of snot leading from his nostril to his lip. He still retained most of this charm now, along with patchy stubble that smelled strange if you got up too close to him. Downstairs in the warehouse his best friend Rizwan, and Tarquin, the new lad, were taking boxes of 'Finest English Fudge' and packing them into empty boxes before sealing and labelling them.

Rizwan's speed wasn't up to his usual standard; normally he came to work in his jeans and an old scruffy t-shirt sporting a chin full of dense black stubble. But today, he was clean shaven and wearing a suit and was being extremely careful not to mess it up. His scrawny, lanky frame was more akin to a long distance runner than a manual labourer but, he was that way due to too much alcohol and drugs rather than a strict dieting regime. The toll of his excess was obvious if you looked closely enough; he was the most pale-skinned Pakistani you'd ever be likely to see.

Fashionably late as usual, Jerry, the office manager and after-work drinking companion of the two, came sauntering over to them. 'All right lads, another good morning packing fudge?' he asked.

This immediately irritated Rizwan. He resented being stuck down on the production line, especially with 'Fudge Packer' as his job title and longed to work upstairs in the offices where he assumed he could do half the work for twice the cash. 'Very funny,' he snapped. 'It's all right for you poncing about in your fucking suit. Now, toddle off upstairs and look important.'

Jerry frowned before looking Rizwan up and down and barking, 'You're wearing a suit too. You fucking knob!'

'Yeah, but with good reason. I've got to go to court today. Remember? Anyway, get yourself off, and don't forget to collect the lottery money. You know what happened last time.'

Jerry walked upstairs in a huff. Of course he knew what happened last time, none of the bastards would ever let him forget. He'd made one mistake and all of a sudden he was the enemy. Anyway, it wasn't just his fault. Nobody came and offered him the money. How was he supposed to know that would be the day the numbers would come up. Obviously, upper management were pleased, they still had their workforce, at least there was some ironic silver lining. As he passed through the door he could hear Tarquin camply shouting, 'Seeee yaaaaa!' at the top of his voice. He chose to ignore him and continued onward to his office.

Tarquin stopped working for a moment, looked at Rizwan and pointed up the stairs toward Jerry's office. 'God, he isn't half a moody bugger first thing on a morning.' Rizwan didn't grace this with a response, he simply carried on packing. After a short period of work, with Tarquin's eyes burning right through him, it seemed pretty obvious to him that an early morning chinwag was expected. There was no way he was going to instigate a conversation though, so he stopped and waited for Tarquin to say something else.

'So,' Tarquin said, 'court, eh? Is it like on telly with all them blokes in the wigs and gowns?'

'It's a courtroom, Tarquin, not a fucking drag act. Anyway it's Magistrates not Crown, so it'll just be a small room with a few guys in posh suits.'

'Are we still going for a drink at *The Nobody* after work?'

Rizwan sighed. He couldn't understand quite why Tarquin always insisted in tagging along when he went to *The Nobody* with Jerry and Clive after work on a

Friday, but, he knew what it was like to be in a minority so often cut him some slack when Jerry started whingeing about it.

'As long as I'm not in prison,' he said.

'Ssshhhh, think positive,' Tarquin was talking with his hands.

This really pissed Rizwan off because it made him look even more gay, if you could get anymore gay that is. It was as if Tarquin was trying his hardest to be a stereotype; flamboyant dyed blonde hair spiked out in all directions, a hint of makeup around his almost feminine features, skinny fit jeans with a pink belt, a woman's Juicy Couture t-shirt that was so tight it looked sprayed on and oversized biker boots on his feet. Rizwan decided that as long as Tarquin didn't try to touch him he'd ignore the gayness and let him finish speaking. 'You'll be fine. I'll see you in the pub after work. Will I be OK for a lift home?'

'We'll see.'

CHAPTER TWO

FRIDAY 8th June – 1 p.m.

Click! Click! 'Beautiful . . . absolutely beautiful . . .' *Click! Click!* 'Come on give it to me! Work it like you mean it! Fantastic . . .' *Click! Click!* 'Come on! I want sex! I want sex appeal!' *Click! Click!* 'I want Reservoir Dogs crossed with Boyzone!' *Click! Click!*

Martin and the rest of the band were trying so hard not to laugh at the photographer's enthusiasm they could barely manage a pose. It was a shame too; they'd gone to so much effort considering the state they'd been in only a few hours earlier. There they were, all dressed up in seventies suits, sporting big lapels and flairs. They even had stick on handlebar moustaches. They looked like something straight out of an old cop show, especially Steve; he was on one knee posing with a replica berretta.

Martin wasn't happy about this; he thought, with him being the front man, he should be the one posing with it, not the drummer. Especially since Steve was the least photogenic of the band, whilst Martin and Jimbob had quite slim frames and boyish features, under the long grunge hair Steve was overweight and had a skinhead.

Martin didn't let it bother him for too long though, he supposed collectively they looked cool. This was their first professional photo shoot and although distracted, they were loving it, despite having been made to wear makeup.

Click! Click! 'Great, that's great!' *Click! Click!* 'Point the gun into lens!' *Click! Click!* 'Come on!' *Click! Click!* 'OK lads, I want you to play an invisible game of twister!'

The choice of props the photographer had decided on was a little strange but seemed to work quite well – an ironing board and a skull added an air of enigma to the already super quirkiness of the images. Each time the camera clicked it would bounce an echo around the wooden walls of the studio.

Jimbob Rifkin had worked hard to get to today. Slogging away since school, they chose the band's name as a mismatch of their own; Jimbob donated his first name and Martin and Steve had donated the first three letters of their surnames, Riffle and Kingsley. They'd been together for around three years and were through to the final of the national under twenty-ones battle of the bands competition. The only other West Yorkshire band to also make it this far was Planet Lounge. Between the two of them they were generating a lot of local interest and were working hard to drum up support for the event; they had two weeks left to shift a pile of tickets. Their schedules were action packed; photo shoots, local newspaper and radio interviews, warm up gigs . . .

It was a shame they hated each other.

Rizwan waited nervously outside the courtroom. He'd just been handed his means form and decided a little bending of the truth might just go his way if they decided to slam him with a fine. He told the truth about his income, they could easily check up and confirm that, but his outgoings were a different matter entirely. They were his business. How were they to know what he did and didn't spend?

As Rizwan came to the part of the form where he had to declare his expenditure, he couldn't help but feel grateful that the court had given him such a varied list of things to put a monthly outgoing amount against. The first box read 'Rent/Mortgage', Riz would never have even thought of putting down a cash figure for rent without their helpful reminder. Since his parents passed away he'd lived rent free at his brothers house. Three hundred pounds sounded about right. Bills? Erm . . . fifty quid. Food? Hundred quid. Cigarettes. Hundred quid. He carried on down the list, fabricating amounts for almost everything. All except one thing, there was a box for alcohol. It could quite easily blow things if he filled that one in.

Completing the form, Rizwan realised that his only real outgoings were petrol and car insurance and was horrified that the only thing he ever had to show for his wages was a hangover, a comedown, or, if he'd gotten lucky, a rather unhealthy dose of the clap. Rizwan had chosen to represent himself, he didn't like solicitors, especially the government funded kind. This way, if he was going to end up getting fucked over, at least he'd only have himself to blame.

'Mr Rizwan, we're ready for you now.' He followed the man who'd called him into the courtroom.

In front of him, on a raised platform, were three guys in posh suits. He presumed one of them must be the judge. There were a couple more suits sitting to the right of the dock. They must be the prosecution. There was also some smarmy-looking twat at the back with a note pad who was probably from the Gazette. He had a brief moment of panic when he realised that if this went in the Gazette, he'd be absolutely fucked. He was going to have to do some pretty sweet talking and super fast thinking to get out of this. Prior to seeing him sitting there, Rizwan would have just taken it on the chin, flogged the car and told his brother he couldn't afford to run it anymore, but if it was plastered all over the paper that he'd been done for drink driving, his brother would kick him out for sure. He'd been looking for an excuse to get rid of him for ages but the house had been left to everyone jointly when his parents died. His brother expected Rizwan to be as serious a Muslim as he was, but the times had changed. If they didn't want him to drink, they shouldn't have brought him up in Yorkshire and sent him to a Church of England school.

Rizwan took another glance around the room and realised that everyone in there, with the exception of him, was white. This could definitely work to his advantage. He stood in the dock and the middle one of the three suits said, 'State your name please.' Rizwan coughed nervously to clear his throat and said, 'Mohammed Rizwan.'

'And I can see you have chosen to represent yourself, Mr Rizwan,' he said flicking through the notes in front of him.

'That's correct. Yes.'

The Judge glanced over at the two guys on Rizwan's right, 'And the charges?'

The one nearest Rizwan stood up. 'On the night of April the twenty-second the defendant was pulled over at approximately ten-thirty for driving without lights. As is standard in this situation, he was breathalysed and at the time it was discovered that Mr Rizwan was over the legal drink drive limit.'

'How do you plead, Mr Rizwan?'

He thought back to the night two weeks prior to this incident; it was a Friday and he'd driven home from *The Nobody* pissed out of his face. He'd pulled up outside his house and misjudged parking the car. Rizwan drove it into a lamp post before he managed to press the brake. He was in that much of a state, he'd just left the car there and staggered into the house and upstairs to bed.

He was woken in the morning by his brother braying loudly at the door in an extremely strong Pakistani accent. 'Wake up, you lazy bastard! Where's the fucking car?' Why was he asking where the car was? It was outside, Rizwan clearly remembered parking it there near perfectly the night before. How his drunk mind lied.

He looked at his brother in confusion and said, 'It's outside!'

Fuming and manic his brother screamed in his face, 'Yes! Wrapped round a fucking lamp post!' Rizwan should have learned his lesson then.

Jimbob Rifkin collectively thanked the photographer. Martin hoped the shots would turn out well; he was surprised at the professionalism of the whole set up. When they were told the competition organisers would be paying for a shoot he assumed it would be some nobody with an instant disposable camera not a posh studio with lighting and long lenses. He'd enjoyed the experience immensely. They all had.

Steve was getting nervous. He hated carrying the gun around, and although it only fired blanks it was highly illegal. He was damned if he was handing it in, though; it had cost him a good few hundred quid. Jimbob, the bass player, wasn't looking forward to the drive home. He wished the other two would pull their finger out and take some lessons, but not only was the local instructor a complete freak, but also Martin seemed to have some kind of weird grudge against him.

The three of them left the studio and piled into Jimbob's Nissan Micra. It was a two hour drive home and they decided between them that a spliff would make the journey a little less painful. As Jimbob pulled the car on to the main road, Martin began to skin up a joint, using the open glove compartment as a tray.

Once onto the main road Jimbob passed his mobile phone back to Steve, 'Here, do us a favour mate.'

'What?'

'Send that bird I shagged earlier a text for me. I want to make sure I don't need to go get checked out for anything.'

Steve wasn't laughing, 'No. Fuck off. Do it yourself,' he said.

'Come on,' said Jimbob, 'It's not like she'll know it's come from you.'

'Fine,' sighed Steve as he began texting, then he slowly repeated the words he was punching in, 'Thanks for last night. Have you got anything that I should get checked out?' He paused, 'Is that OK do you reckon? It sounds a bit harsh.'

'Yeah. Maybe your right,' said Jimbob. 'Put a kiss on the end of it.'

'Where the fuck did you get that gun?' interrupted Jimbob.

'I've had it years,' replied Steve. 'You used to be able to buy them all over the place until the law got stupid. It fires blanks but it's well loud. It sounds real.'

'It fucking looks real. It's no wonder they were made illegal. You could easily get away with doing a robbery or something with that. Nobody would know it's a replica.'

'Not guilty.'

The judge looked at Rizwan in confusion and disbelief before saying, 'So you are saying, Mr Rizwan, that on the night in question, you didn't drink any alcohol?'

'That's correct, sir. I am.'

As the words left his mouth, he remembered the week

after. He'd decided to leave the car at home that night and share a taxi with Clive instead. On his way back, the driver was having a go at them because they'd both bought kebabs which were stinking the car out. He'd made them wrap them back up and had banned them from eating in his cab. Rizwan had the driver drop him at the top of the street so his brother couldn't see him and walked the rest of the way, well, staggered. But, as he got to the door, he realised his family were all still up. There was no way he was going inside in such a state, he was too far gone to pretend to be sober. Rizwan decided it would be a good idea to go and wait in his car. He got in, sat down, and immediately fell asleep, dropping his kebab all over the passenger seat.

A couple of hours later he woke up wondering where he was. Once he'd realised, he glanced over to the house and could see they'd all gone to bed. Nice one. Now he could get back in unnoticed. He opened the car door, stood up to get out, automatically pushing down the door lock and closing the car door. The door was swirling around in the distance; it reminded him of the dancing lady in the opening credits of Roald Dahl's *Tales of the Unexpected*. She was taunting him, daring him to try and make it.

Rizwan paused for a moment to gather some self-control, gave himself a quick slap around the face and went for it, clumsily zig-zagging as he stumbled towards the door, fumbling around in his pockets for his key. He was panting as if he'd run a marathon and had to search for a good few minutes before realising he must have left the keys in the bastard car. Un . . . believable!

He glanced back across the road. The car looked even further away than the door had just been. He braced himself and quickly wobbled his way back. Once there, Rizwan pushed his face up against the glass and peered through the passenger side window. His keys were there, on the front seat next to the spilled out kebab. Surprisingly the kebab looked inviting and his dry, dehydrated mouth began to salivate. The urge to eat the abandoned kebab, combined with the urge to get in the house gave him a sudden, but overwhelming, burst of motivation. He tried all the doors but they were locked. In his infinite pissed-up wisdom he decided there was only one option. He stooped, grabbed the first stone he saw and made his way back to the passenger side, where he threw the stone full force at the window. It bounced straight back at him, and struck him hard on the end of his nose. Although he could barely see through the tears which had instantly pricked his eyes, he found it absolutely hilarious. Note to self . . . bigger brick. Then he saw it. Spot on. He picked it up, took three steps back and launched it through the glass. Bingo. Mission accomplished.

Now he was pissed off. He'd been really looking forward to polishing off that kebab but, to his dismay, there were shards of glass all over it, and on reflection, to add to the already expansive list of things he should have done differently that evening: he really wished he'd ordered chicken. He cursed himself, picked out his keys then staggered back across the road, let himself in and trundled upstairs to bed.

In the morning, regular as clockwork, his brother brayed at the door and began shouting. 'Wake up, you lazy Bastard! I need you to drive me to work!' Luckily he was almost ready. He'd been in that much of a state the previous night that he'd not even managed to get undressed. He grabbed his piece of emergency chewing gum, chewed furiously for a couple of seconds and opened the door. 'I'm ready. Chill out.'

He followed his brother down the stairs and outside to the car. 'I don't fucking believe it!' his brother shouted.

'What?' asked Rizwan.

'Somebody has broken into the car!' Rizwan looked genuinely horrified. Not because of what his brother had just said, but because he suddenly remembered what he'd done the night before. It was time for some quick thinking.

'You're joking,' Rizwan said. 'Why would anybody do that? Why? Why!'

His brother peered quizzically in to the car before yelling, 'The dirty bastards! They've left a kebab on the front seat!'

Rizwan had decided there and then that in future, it would be far simpler to drink and drive. This incident had only served to prove to him that even when he tried to do the right thing, everything went pear-shaped anyway. *This* was why he felt suitably justified when he looked the judge straight in the eyes and said.

'The only thing I can think is that my drinks must have been spiked. I was only in the pub because one of my friends needed a lift home. Because I'm a devout Muslim and do not drink, he knew I would definitely be OK to drive. I felt a bit funny when I left the pub but I just assumed it was something I had eaten. Because I've never been drunk before, how was I supposed to know how it feels? I'd had five glasses of coke whilst I was in the pub and they must have been tampered with. I am as shocked and disgusted as you are.' He was impressed with his lie and hoped it would cut the mustard.

The Judge stroked his chin thoughtfully and then looked at the guys either side of him. They exchanged a couple of whispers. Rizwan couldn't help but think he might have over-egged the pudding. The Judge looked at Rizwan and said, 'I'd like to ask you to take a seat outside whilst we consider what you've said and determine our course of action.'

Was this good news or bad news? Was this normal procedure? Rizwan didn't remember anybody else that morning having to wait outside. He walked calmly out of the courtroom, hoping and praying he'd not blown it, then took the same seat he'd sat in previously and began biting his nails.

He wasn't waiting long before he heard, 'Mr Rizwan, we're ready for you now.' By the time Rizwan turned to acknowledge the voice, whoever had called him had disappeared back inside. As he walked back to the dock he wondered which of the two men sitting either side of the judge had owned the mysterious disappearing voice.

'In light of what you've said, Mr Rizwan, we are willing to take you at your word this time. However, we cannot dismiss the fact that you were driving without your lights on and because of this we have no option but to charge you with driving without due care and attention. We will endorse your driving license with three penalty points. In view of your personal financial circumstances we'll fine you a fixed sum of sixty pounds. We also insist that you take an advanced driver training course next week.'

'Thank you,' mumbled Rizwan. He was dying to laugh out loud so hard he had to bite his lip and cough. Funny thing was though, the Judge seemed to think he was doing this to stop himself crying.

'There's no need to get upset, Mr Rizwan. You'll have nothing to worry about as long as you never show your face in my courtroom again. If you're as sincere as you appear to be, this is where the discomfort ends. But, if you appear before me again in similar circumstances and it transpires that you have deceived me on this occasion, I will have absolutely no hesitation in imposing a custodial sentence.'

They were only half way down the spliff but Jimbob was really seriously considering it. Had the buzz of playing worn off so much he needed to find excitement by going to such extremes? He was verbally pondering, 'We couldn't do it anywhere near here . . . or anywhere near home for that matter. We'd have to go somewhere else. Somewhere neutral.'

The other two were giggling at how seriously he was thinking it through. Neither of them stopped him rambling, it was too entertaining.

'And, it couldn't be anything too big, like a bank. We'd definitely get fucked if we turned over a bank. Post offices are a no no; they're full of C.C.T.V. and shit. Bookies? No. No they won't do either. I've seen *Eastenders*, bookies are all run by gangsters. It'd have to be a . . . erm . . . corner shop or something. Yeah, a corner shop. What do you think, lads?'

'I think you're a fucking head case!' said Martin.

Jimbob was taken aback, had they been joking when

they'd suggested a robbery? Who cares! Even i
been joking, he wasn't, it sounded like a right bu
It was your idea in the first place.'

Martin spoke slowly and moved his hands to mime sign
language, 'It. Was. A. Joke!'

'I'm not laughing. I think we should do it. It'll be
funny,' said Jimbob.

Steve had stopped laughing now, this was turning into
no laughing matter. He moved across to the middle of
the back seat and leaned forward, his head popped out
between the front seats like a tortoise that had just smelled
a tasty lettuce and he glanced at Jimbob. 'You're not
serious are you, Jimmy boy? It won't be funny when you're
in prison being bummed by some massive black guy!'

'Rubbish!' snapped Jimbob. 'Even if we did get caught,
which we won't, it'd take a lot more than a small corner
shop robbery to end up in jail being Big Bubba's bitch.
Stop being such a fadge!'

Martin thought it best that he try to diffuse the situation. 'Why are you two even arguing about this? It's not
like we're actually going to do it.'

Jimbob couldn't believe they were being so completely
wet. 'Come on, you two, stop being such a pair of fannies.
If you're that bothered, I'll hold the gun. Then, if we did
get caught, which like I said, we won't, it'll be me that
cops all the flack for it.'

Martin was slowly becoming convinced that this might actually be an interesting way to spend the afternoon, but Steve's mind set hadn't changed and he shouted, 'The answer is no!'

Martin decided it might be a good time to work some of his magic on Steve, it was time to get his selling head on. 'Steve, let me ask you a question. We've done some pretty amazing things in our time, the three of us. We've known each other since primary school and that's a long time. When we started sixth form we formed the band so we could get free booze in pubs when we were under age and shag birds, and it worked. We've lived it large, we've tried every drug under the sun. We've been involved in many brawls and always won. We're golden. Anything we set our minds to we can achieve, and as we've demonstrated in the past, there's some things we've tried just for the sake of trying them, realised it was a bad idea and never bothered trying again. That doesn't matter though, because I think we're all in agreement with the fact that, out of everything we've done in the past, even the incredibly stupid stuff, we've never regretted a thing. In fact, we're proud of all of it. So my question to you, Steve, is this; do you want to look back later in life and regret never having tried this, or do you want to look back proud and think, "Jesus Christ, that was fucking mental!"?'

Sold.

CHAPTER THREE

FRIDAY 8th June – 4 p.m.

A strange looking middle-aged man called Brian had a spring in his step and a smile as wide as his huge moustache as he excitedly strutted towards *Jonny T's Autos*. He knew he'd have to put up with a barrage of verbal abuse from the owner, but Tourette's was involuntary, not abusive, and at the end of the day, there wasn't another garage in Holme Bridge that could do a better deal. There wasn't another garage in Holme Bridge full stop. A bit of verbal abuse was a small price to pay, and anyway, he couldn't feel negative on a day like today. It had taken what seemed like an eternity of hard work and saving for this day to come to fruition and he wasn't going to let a few fucks and twats ruin it.

He approached the car lot and looked up at the sign, '*Jonny T's Autos* – If I Call You A Bastard It's Not My Fault,' then smiled to himself and patiently waited for Jonny to come to his assistance, which he promptly did.

He walked confidently over to Brian, placed a firm hand on his shoulder and said, 'Now then *fucking twat*, what can I get for you today?' He didn't even give Brian a chance to respond before he started ranting, 'Something sporty? A saloon? Family man are you? *Twat, fuck, spunk!* Or maybe a *bastard*, sorry *shit*, sorry *clit*, sorry . . . van?'

Brian smiled and began the speech he'd rehearsed in his mind over the last few months in preparation for this moment. 'I require an automobile fit for only the finest and most proficient of drivers. A machine that will match my intellect and superior co-ordination whilst furnishing me with the capability to improve my already near perfect driving skills.'

Jonny was gob smacked. It was usually him that caused people to be dumbstruck. He looked at Brian confused and bemused. 'You fucking what?'

Then Brian smiled, and feeling proud and bold he returned Jonny's 'hand on shoulder' gesture and proclaimed, 'I require a one point eight Mondeo.'

As Jimbob Rifkin finished hunting the back streets of Blackpool looking for suitable targets, they all shared the same unspoken feelings on what they were here to do; it was definitely a bad idea, no question, but having come this far, they were fucked if they were not going to go through with it.

They had scoped out a few possible shops and narrowed it down to two. They were both tucked well out of the way and seemed to mainly service local businesses, one was near some office blocks, and the other near some industrial units. They'd decided that they should wait a few hours to make their move, as both shops would probably double the amount they had in the till between five and six when everybody was rushing out of work. They also figured that because of the locations, there would be very few customers around to potentially witness the crime after half past six; nobody likes to work late on a Friday.

Jimbob had been inside the one near the industrial units to check it out, no cameras and no nooks and crannies. It was definitely the safest of the two, as the shop was laid out in such a way that the owner could see every shelf. It was completely open plan. They were obviously a lot more concerned about spotting shop-lifters than having a gun shoved in their mouth.

Martin had checked out the one near the office blocks. This one was a little more complex, it still didn't have any cameras, but it was extremely cluttered, about five small aisles stocking everything from Snickers to sanitary towels.

The decision they had to make was a simple one; go for

the safe, first option or take a gamble on the second. They knew the second one would bring in more money, providing they didn't bank half their takings after lunch, because it incorporated a sandwich bar.

Either way, they had already discussed that going in there with a Yorkshire accent would leave too much of a trail. After trying a few different accents out in the car they decided to go for sounding like Scousers. They'd decided that this would work out well for two reasons; firstly, the Liverpool accent was distinctive and very easy to do and secondly, they thought that if anybody was likely to rob somewhere in Blackpool, it would more than likely be a Scouser.

They also knew that they had to cover their faces. They needed some masks from somewhere. Fortunately, with this being a seaside town they didn't even have to go to the risk of buying them from a shop. Just split up for a couple of hours whilst they waited for the offices or factories to clear out and trawl the arcades looking for machines that had them as prizes, if you were nimble enough with the controls of a mechanical claw.

In a small flat that looked out over the council estates, a mentally challenged young man was sat on a sofa cuddling his best friend. Paul and Theodore loved this time of day. It was when all of the best television was on. Paul really enjoyed watching CITV with his tea on his lap. Theodore didn't eat though, he'd told Paul it was because he was magic and Paul had believed him. Why wouldn't he? Theodore was there to look out for him. For almost fifteen years he'd watched his back and made sure he was all right.

If it wasn't for Theodore telling him what to do, they'd still be in that horrible hospital eating plastic tasting food and going for endless consultations with shiny faced blokes who didn't know what they were talking about. Eventually Theodore decided it was time for them to get out. He told Paul exactly what to say and do and it worked.

Now they had this nice flat and they got money from the post office every couple of weeks. It had worked out quite well. Theodore helped Paul with everything. He'd even helped him through taking his first tentative steps towards building a social life by encouraging him to go to the pub. He was accepted at *The Nobody Inn* now – well, at least by a few of them. He went every day at opening time and again at seven o' clock once *The Simpsons* had finished.

In the damp darkness of the room they were confined to, one thing that Billy and Bobby had plenty of, was time. In fact it was pretty much all they had. Sure, they were fed and given water but they longed to see what life was like beyond the room. At the same time, they had overwhelming feelings of agoraphobia and dread at the prospect of what might await them if they were to break free. Perhaps they were being kept there for a reason. Perhaps they were being protected from something. Contrary thoughts passed their minds and occasionally their mouths, not that they really needed to talk all that much. There was little to talk about, conversation points were severely lacking. They had a secret, though. They knew something that that their captors did not. Underneath an old barrel in the corner were the beginnings of a tunnel.

They were blessed with a bit of good fortune around a year ago when they managed to steal a spoon and it went unnoticed when they returned their empty bowls. It didn't even resemble a spoon any more, it looked more like a coin. A year's worth of digging had taken its toll and despite their best efforts, they'd never managed to get themselves another one. A window of opportunity was approaching shortly, though, they'd get their hands on something useful. The hole would take them an eternity to finish otherwise. Even after all this time, it was only just wide and deep enough for them to get an arm in up to the elbow.

CHAPTER FOUR

FRIDAY 8th June – 6 p.m.

Clive, Jerry and Tarquin had been in *The Nobody Inn* since they finished work at S-packers an hour and a half earlier, and were already well on their way to being legless. They were all quietly concerned that Rizwan might have been sent down because they hadn't heard anything from him since he left work for court earlier that morning. Their various concerns were for fundamentally different reasons; Tarquin, although he didn't know Rizwan all that well, didn't want to be bored at work, and even though Rizwan was an Asian, he was all right company. Being Riz's best friend, Clive was genuinely concerned for him, he also felt more than slightly bothered that without him he'd be severely short of friends because Rizwan stuck up for him. Jerry was concerned because he wouldn't be able to tap him up for a lift anymore and he'd have to start recruiting to fill his position. But, more importantly, it was just about time for another round and Jerry realised that if Rizwan turned up now it'd be his turn to get them in. He glanced at his watch and said, 'Where is that fucking fudge packer?'

Tarquin glanced at Jerry from across the table and said, 'I'm sat here, in front of you. You ginger tool.'

Jerry was quick to snap back, 'Not you, you fucking arse bandit. The one that does it for a job, not a sexual preference!' Clive had turned around and was staring out of the window. 'Dunno,' he said, 'it might rain you know, it's getting dark outside.' As the words left Clive's mouth Rizwan strolled into the pub and headed towards the table. Jerry stood up, arm outstretched to shake Rizwan's hand and said, 'It's just got dark in here too! Now then, it's the Pakistani Oliver Reed, how you doing?'

Rizwan shook his hand, made a remark about Jerry being fat and ginger and said, 'Cause for a celebration, lads. I got off with a fine, some points and a poxy driving course.' They broke into a round of applause then Jerry said, 'I'll drink to that. Are you getting them in then, Riz?' Rizwan sighed and turned around to head to the bar but Clive interrupted.

'You sit down Riz, we're celebrating. I'll get them in. Stellas all round?' The group nodded their approval. He hadn't chosen to get a round in for their sakes, he'd chosen to get one in because Doreen had just started work behind the bar and he thought he might be able to pluck up the courage to ask her out. Funny thing is though, Tarquin was convinced Clive was in the closet and was determined to drag him out of it, kicking and screaming if necessary.

Clive approached the bar and, in an effort to look casual, rested his elbow on it. This didn't work as planned because he put it in some spilled beer. He quickly assessed the situation; did he pull his arm quickly away and run the risk of looking stupid, or simply leave his elbow in the beer and hope Doreen didn't notice? He opted for the latter. He tried to speak but the words wouldn't come out. His mouth was getting dryer by the second and his cheeks were burning up. It felt as if someone was holding an invisible hairdryer to his face. He decided a smile would buy him a couple of seconds, then rehearsed the drinks order in his mind before hesitantly saying, 'Hiya Doreen,' Clive was more nervous than a ten-year-old girl at a Garry Glitter concert, so nervous, that he couldn't tell Doreen was feeling exactly the same. 'Hiya Clive,' she replied.

Over at the table Jerry was trying to squeeze out some detail of the court case in an effort to build up a bank of piss-take ammunition to use on Rizwan when the opportunity arose. 'So, how the fuck did you blag not getting a ban then?' he asked.

'Played the race card,' replied Rizwan.

'How do you mean?' Jerry asked, puzzled.

'Well, I'm a Muslim, aren't I?'

'Are you?'

'Yeah, course I am you fucking spaz,' Rizwan snapped.

'I thought you were a Paki.'

'I am, you racist twat, but I'm also a Muslim.'

'I'm not getting you.'

Rizwan sighed in disbelief at Jerry's stupidity. 'Muslim is a religion, Jerry, not a nationality. Like Jews.'

'Yeah, they're Jewish. Still not getting you.'

'And where do Jews come from, Jerry? Jew isn't a place.'

'Yeah, but I just thought they came from somewhere that didn't link to their name, like the Dutch coming from Holland.'

Rizwan flopped back in his chair, shook his head and said, 'Are you taking the piss?'

Jerry leaned towards him and smiled. 'Course I am, you bell-end, so what did you say?'

Rizwan chuckled as he explained what had gone on and how the Gazette reporter could have made things difficult. This left Tarquin with a few questions. 'So,' he asked, 'if you are a Muslim, then how come you drink in the first place?'

'What religion are you two?' he asked, glancing between them. 'Catholic? Christian? Or some shit like that?'

They nodded.

Rizwan pointed at Tarquin. 'You're a faggot,' he glanced at Jerry. 'And you're definitely not a virgin, so neither of you two stick to your religions. Anyway, I'm pretty strict in other ways. I still go to the mosque on occasions, I stick to the rules at Ramadan, I only eat Halal meat, I don't eat pork and I will eventually go to Mecca.'

'Mecca,' said Jerry, 'What the fuck will you go there for?'

'Every Muslim has to go at least once in their lifetime, you need to go to get into heaven.'

The next thing Jerry said took Rizwan completely by surprise. 'I'll go with you if you want.'

'Really?' asked Rizwan. 'Why?'

'I haven't been to bingo for ages, it's full of scratty up-for-it birds.'

As all three of them burst out laughing, Tarquin saw the chemistry between Clive and Doreen through the corner of his eye and didn't like it, but he was amused by the fact that neither of them were managing to speak to each other. Clive panicked, the drink order had completely left his brain. There he was, all doe-eyed and soggy-elbowed, without the first idea of what drinks he should be ordering. He was so busy trying not to stare at her model-like angular features that his eyes dropped to her modest but perfect breasts. It took a moment for him to register that this would definitely be a worse place to stare and decided to look her straight in the eyes. Unfortunately, as he did he got lost in them, they were hypnotic; such a dark brown that they almost appeared black. He forgot completely where he was and what he was supposed to be doing but thankfully Doreen rescued him. 'Four pints of Stella, is it?' she asked, but before he could answer Tarquin stormed over, barged him out of the way and said, 'And four aftershocks as well, please, love.'

If looks could kill, Tarquin would have impaled her with an extraordinarily large skewer, making a massive Doreen kebab right there behind the bar. Clive tried to push his way back in front of Tarquin but he wouldn't budge. He turned to him, smiled and said, 'You go sit down, Clive, I'll bring these over.'

Clive tried to speak, justify why he should be there, but Tarquin physically turned him around and gently pushed him towards the table before throwing Doreen another icy stare. 'And a tray please, love.'

As Clive sat back down at the table Riz leaned over and warned, 'I think you'd better watch your arse. Tarquin seems to have taken a bit of a shine to you.' Jerry and Riz cracked up laughing but, Clive didn't find it in the least bit funny. As their amusement subsided Tarquin returned to the table with a tray full of drinks. He passed a pint to each of them and put all four Aftershocks in front of

Rizwan, who looked at Tarquin and asked, 'What the fuck do you expect me to do with them?'

Before Tarquin could answer Jerry barked, 'Drink 'em you soft bastard. You've got some catching up to do.'

Rizwan picked up the first small shot glass and threw the Aftershock down his throat. It burned and made his eyes water, he hoped the rest would be easier to swallow. Clive couldn't watch, he excused himself and headed off to the toilet. He was followed closely by Tarquin. Jerry made eye contact with Riz and said, 'I think you were right, he's following him to the loo.' Rizwan smiled and fired down his second Aftershock, it was even worse than the first and he struggled to stop it coming back up as quickly as it went down. Searching for a ploy to delay drinking the other two he said, 'You better give me your lottery money before you fucking spend it. If you remembered to collect it. Remember what happened? Four million quid. FOUR MILLION QUID! Just think what we'd be doing now if you'd put 'em on.'

Jerry reached into his pocket and pulled out a small wad of notes. 'All right. No need to declare a fucking jihad,' he said as he passed them over to Rizwan. Clive was on his way back from the toilet looking anxious. He reached the table and sat down quietly; his hands trembled as he picked up his pint of Stella.

'A fucking jihad!' Rizwan said frustrated, 'Why do you

constantly fucking mock me? If you're so fucking racist, why not just drink with someone else.'

Jerry sighed and flopped his shoulders. 'I'm not racist,' he said, 'not in the least, it's just banter. I love you really. It's like when you used to pull the girl you fancied's pigtails when you were little. Except not in a gay way.'

'Well, fair enough, but jihad? For fuck's sake. I hate wars and violence and all that bollocks.'

'I think they're great,' Clive piped in. Jerry and Rizwan froze mid conversation and turned their heads. 'You what?' asked Jerry, concerned.

'War films,' said Clive, 'I think they're great.' Jerry and Rizwan sighed and relaxed as Clive continued, 'What were that one with all the cool music in? Erm ... Pontoon, that's it, Pontoon.'

Behind the bar, Dave had taken charge and had had a go at Doreen because the bar top was covered in spilled beer. He'd decided to send her to wash up in the kitchen where she couldn't cause as much carnage. Best place for her if you asked him. Stupid cow. He scanned the room looking for imperfections and it didn't take him long to find one. He reached under the bar and pulled out a child's Spiderman walkie talkie, depressed the button on the side and hollered into it. 'Shirley!'

Shirley heard his voice booming from the left side pocket, third up, of her apron; she was struggling to carry a crate of Budweiser up the cellar stairs. She stopped immediately, pressed the crate against the wall and pushed her knee up to balance it, freeing a hand. She pulled out the walkie talkie and said, 'Yes love?' There was a short pause before Dave's voice crackled through the speaker, 'Empty glasses, table four!'

She carefully put the walkie talkie back into its holster in her apron, secured the crate and lowered her leg before struggling up the rest of the stairs. Once behind the bar, she placed the heavy crate down and walked past Dave to collect the empty glasses from Jerry's table.

As she picked up the empties, Tarquin surfaced from the toilet and took his seat next to a still uncomfortable Clive. Shirley had managed to collect all four empty shot glasses in one hand and the three pint glasses in the other. She was heading back to the bar when she heard, 'Shirley!' coming from the walkie talkie. She carefully placed all the empty glasses onto the vacant table next to the lads, grabbed the walkie talkie, plunged the button on the side and said, 'Yes love?'

'Is this fucking crate going to sit here all night?'

Whilst all this had been happening, there was a fully grown man standing outside *The Nobody* wearing a pair of Superman pyjamas, a towelling dressing gown and big fluffy tiger feet slippers. He held a small teddy bear. He'd been there for quite a while before walking into the pub.

Nobody seemed to notice as he approached the bar to order a drink, nobody that is except Jerry, who said, 'Right lads, come on let's sup up and fuck off. I can't drink in comfort with that spacker in here.'

In the cramped confines of Jimbob Rifkin's Nissan Micra the nerves were starting to show and the conversation was getting a little heated. 'Look, Steve!' shouted Jimbob. 'I know it was my fucking idea but I need to be out here running the engine. You can't expect me to come in there with you and then piss around starting the car once we've finished. We need to vanish as soon as you run out of there. What if they see the car?'

Steve couldn't believe that after talking them into this, he was just going to sit outside in the car while they did all the hard work. 'You've taken off the registration plates!' he shouted, 'There must be a fucking million maroon Micras go through Blackpool every day.'

Martin could see both sides of the argument. He was pissed off that Jimbob wouldn't be inside with them too; it meant that he'd have to be the one waving the gun around. There was no way Steve would do it. On the other hand, if either of them had got off their arses and taken driving lessons the situation would be entirely different. He decided to mediate. 'Listen you two, it just means we'll have to do the other shop. The open plan one, it's not like we need three of us in there. There's no aisles for people to be hiding in.'

Then Steve said something that surprised both of them. He decided that he'd come this far and there was no point in prolonging things. It was time for him to 'rip off the plaster' as his mum used to say. 'Look,' he said, 'bollocks to it. If we're going to do it let's just do it here and do it now. I want to go home.'

Jimbob was parked just outside the shop and nobody had been in or out for the last few minutes. Although Steve wasn't happy about what they were doing, he did realise that this window of opportunity had made the more difficult shop the place to do it.

They went over the routine one more time before Jimbob pulled the car just around the corner from the shop, where he could quickly exit on to the main road. Martin picked up the gun and tucked it into the front of his trousers, emptied the seventies suit out of the Tesco carrier bag holding it and stuffed the bag into his back pocket, then he and Steve put on the masks, ran around the corner and entered the shop.

Steve dropped the Yale lock and turned the 'Open' sign to 'Closed' as they walked in. Scouse accent at the ready, Martin withdrew the gun and pointed it straight at the owner before casually and calmly saying, 'Put your fuckin' hands up, mate.' The shop keeper raised his hands and Steve ran around to make sure nobody else was lurking in the isles.

Martin pulled the carrier bag from his pocket, placed it on the counter and said in an American trying to sound like the Beatles in a bad biopic tone, 'Open the till and put all the money into that bag.' He was impressed with how well he was managing to keep his cool; he knew he must be doing a convincing job because the shop keeper just stood there shocked and frozen, partly terrified and partly confused. This threw Martin off centre and there was an uncomfortable silence. He was starting to get annoyed, his Darth Vader mask was warm. *It's no wonder he breathed so loud in Star Wars*, he thought; *he must have been sweating his knackers off.* His patience ran out so he decided to give the shop keeper a little bit more encouragement and shouted, 'Now!'

Steve returned to the front of the counter and said, 'It's clear.' This irritated Martin even more. The prick had forgotten to say it in a scouse accent.

The shop keeper opened the till and shaking, he started to remove the cash and place it in the bag, Martin realised he should have instructed the guy to do it with one hand, he could grab anything with the other. Just to make sure the owner didn't get any funny ideas, he shoved the gun right into his face. This hurried things along a bit, but Martin was still getting more and more annoyed. 'The fucking notes! Not the fucking coins!'

The shop keeper obliged. Once all of the notes had been emptied, Martin picked up the bag and waved the gun, motioning the shop keeper out from behind the counter. 'OK, I want you to lie face down on the floor and put your hands behind your back.' The shop keeper anxiously did as he was told; Martin kept the gun firmly fixed on him, trying with all his strength to keep his arm and his hand from wobbling uncontrollably with the nerves.

He glanced over at a Chewbacca-mask-wearing Steve and said, 'Open the door and check outside.' Steve carefully, silently unlocked the Yale, peered through the door and whispered, 'All clear.'

This pissed Martin off further. That time he did have a Scouse accent. Martin turned his attention back to the shop keeper. 'Right. Count to fifty and get up, believe me if we leave here and cops are following us, you'll end up dead!' As he saw the shop keeper's reaction, he was impressed at the authority he must have shown and was more confident of a clean getaway.

Martin and Steve turned on their heel, ran from the shop and around the corner. Jimbob was there, engine running, ready and waiting, he threw open the passenger door and flung down the seat to provide a swift entrance to the rear. Martin jumped in and pulled the seat back, leaving Steve with the easy job of jumping in and closing the door.

Jimbob put his foot down and burned away. 'Why the fuck was the registration plate back on the car?' asked Steve.

'Because,' replied Jimbob, 'while you were in there I decided it probably wouldn't be a good idea to be making a getaway with no reg plate. Get your masks off and once we're on the main road, I'll drive like an angel. I can't get pulled if I'm doing nowt wrong.'

Martin agreed, 'It's a good point, Steve, he's probably done the right thing.'

'I was thinking as well,' said Jimbob, 'we need to get rid of your clothes and those masks, burn them if you need to.'

That was something they hadn't thought about. They both wished they'd worn some crappy clothes instead of their expensive gear. Not that it mattered; they could easily replace their outfits with the cash they'd just robbed. Martin removed his mask and began counting their loot; almost fifteen hundred pounds.

The enormity of what they'd just done was hitting Steve pretty hard. He'd removed his mask and was sat there quietly with his head in his hands. His once tanned and healthy looking face was now drained of colour and beads of cold sweat were appearing on his brow. Jimbob just wanted the details, 'What happened then?'

Martin stopped counting, 'It was too fucking easy, man . . . well easy. Went like clockwork.'

Jimbob felt guilty for instigating the whole thing. He needed that money though; he worked for the local night-club owner knocking out pills and grams of coke, but over the last few months, he'd been munching and snorting his way through as much of the stuff as he'd been selling. He owed two grand and hoped to God that they'd got enough from this job to take the heat off him for long enough to find the rest. They wouldn't make it as rock and roll stars if he had no knee caps.

CHAPTER FIVE

FRIDAY 8th June - 11 p.m.

Jerry's house was a short drive around the corner from the pub. It was at the posh end of Holme Bridge and was one of four houses on a plot of land called 'The Copse' that used to be a farm. His modern taste in interior furnishings was the complete opposite of how the old barn looked on the outside and seemed to have a strong feminine touch for a bloke that lived alone and had little respect for women. The giveaway clue to his singledom was a faint aroma of old washing, the takeaway cartons that seemed to litter more than their fair share of floor space and the magazine rack full of porn in the toilet.

As was customary after a Friday night's drinking, Rizwan, Clive, himself and more recently Tarquin, were all a bit worse for wear. Too much alcohol combined with a smattering of Jimbob's freshly delivered cocaine and copious amounts of marijuana had left them incapable of even the most basic of motor functions; their vision was blurred and their speech was slurred. This wasn't going to stop them, though; they carried on undeterred. They'd each just cracked open another can of Stella and Tarquin was building a joint the size of a Cuban cigar which contained a lot more pot than tobacco. He looked up briefly and reminded them that somebody would have to replace the money and go put the lottery syndicate on tomorrow because they'd blown the cash on half an ounce of skunk and an eighth of coke. Rizwan and Clive were just about managing to play a football game on the X-box and they were all in the midst of a stoned-up giggle fit.

Even though Jerry was in a similar state to the rest of them, he realised he wasn't the centre of attention anymore and said, 'Why do we always end up back here? We should be out pulling birds.' he glanced at Tarquin, 'Except you.'

'What's wrong with chilling out, getting wasted and playing video games?' asked Clive.

'Fucking sad, that's why. Video games prey on impressionable minds,' replied Jerry.

'Shut up!' Rizwan piped in. 'If Pac Man had affected our generation we'd all be dancing around in darkened rooms listening to repetitive music munching on pills.'

They all laughed before Jerry blurted, 'Seriously though, let's go pull some fanjita!'

Clive responded, but kept both eyes firmly fixed on the television screen. 'What are you on about? I wouldn't go

near half the birds you've shagged. They're all minging!'
Another minor chorus of laughter ensued.

'At least I've actually shagged a bird, you fucking
virgin.' Chuckles progressed to full blown laughter from
all except Clive, who quickly defended himself. 'I'm not.
I've shagged loads.'

Through the laughter Rizwan managed to ask, 'Oh,
yeah. Who?'

Clive paused the game, much to Riz's annoyance.
'Nobody you'd know. Don't you remember me telling you
about that bird on holiday?'

Jerry responded, 'Oh, yeah. Imagine.'

Clive snapped straight back, 'Imogene, you twat!'

They started laughing again but Riz started to feel guilty
and jumped to his friend's defence. 'At the end of the day
Jerry. I'd rather be a virgin like Clive than shag some of
the birds you've had.'

Jerry jumped on this, 'Why, what's wrong with 'em?'

Pleased that he was no longer the butt of the joke, Clive
took the game off pause and said, 'The last one looked like
an alien.'

Tarquin stopped building the half finished spliff and
corrected Clive, 'She looked like an ugly 'un.'

'Yeah a big, fat ugly 'un,' Clive agreed.

They'd clearly rattled Jerry, 'Oh fuck off you lot. You're
all wankers.'

Riz felt a tiny twinge of guilt and offered a couple of words of support, 'Only joking, mate. I'd have shagged her.'

Pleased and relieved, Jerry managed a smile and seeking further reassurance he mumbled, 'Would you?'

Rizwan didn't feel all that guilty though, 'Yeah,' he replied, 'from behind.'

'Fuck off, you fucking black bastard!' yelled Jerry.

''Ere, you can't fucking say that.' said Rizwan defensively.

'Why not?'

'We had this conversation earlier. It's racist.'

'So fucking what! You call me a fat ginger bastard all the time.'

'That's different.'

'Why?'

'Because you are.'

'And you're fucking black!'

'No I'm not! I'm an Asian.'

'All right then. You're a fucking brown bastard.'

'I'm not even brown. I'm more like beige.'

Jerry began laughing hysterically, the others turned to glance at him not seeing the joke.

'What's so funny?' asked Tarquin.

Jerry tried to control his breathing and said, 'He's a fucking Basian!'

CHAPTER SIX

FRIDAY 15th June – 8 a.m.

Dave was sitting in his armchair, finishing off his perfect cup of tea and eating his perfect bacon sandwich; white bread with the crusts trimmed off, lightly toasted but only on the inside, thinly buttered with Lurpac and containing three rashers of bacon, crispy, but only the nice meaty rounded part. The straggly end bit and all of the fat had been carefully removed and the sandwich was cut diagonally into exact halves, Shirley had used a protractor. It was served with a tablespoon of Heinz tomato ketchup which was placed neatly on the side. On the table next to him were two anniversary cards. Inside Shirley's was a brief report, outlining the effort and attainment levels she'd reached throughout the previous year. Dave had awarded her an overall score of C-. Shirley came to collect his empty cup but before she could pick it up Dave grabbed her by the waist and pulled her onto his knee.

'Shirley my darling.' He took her hand, gently kissed

it and looked lovingly into her eyes. 'Rarely do I show you the appreciation or the thanks you deserve for helping me in this job and now, after fourteen years of marriage, I've decided to buy an extra special present for you.'

Shirley was overcome by his proclamation; it was so entirely out of character. Finally, after fourteen years of measuring and polishing, he'd cracked. She'd always felt that if she persevered for long enough she would be rewarded with a glimpse of the loving husband that was hidden beneath his obsessive compulsive exterior. She thought back to the pain she'd endured and numerous daily lectures she'd received. It hadn't all been bad though. She'd be lying if she said the sex was anything other than mind-blowing, though she had always found his wild abandon strangely paradoxical. Her chin began to quiver and her eyes welled up. 'Oh Dave.'

'Shirley, I've been concerned that I'm putting you under too much pressure, your work's been suffering lately and I can't help but think I'm slightly at fault, so I've decided to burn the manuals.'

Struggling to contain her emotions, she lifted up the bottom of her apron to mop her leaking eyes. 'Oh Dave, this means so much to me, thank you. thank you.'

'Yes. After thought and careful consideration I decided it was time for them to go. And that's not all.' He let go of her hand and delved into her apron pocket, pulling out the walkie talkie before throwing it across the room. Then he reached into his top shirt pocket, removed a small round object and carefully placed it into Shirley's ear. She looked confused.

'Shirley, I've replaced them with a far more intricate and sophisticated C.C.T.V. system covering every inch of the pub and the car park. I didn't allow you to come into the office because I've been having the monitors fitted and I didn't want to ruin the surprise. Now I can simply sit upstairs and deliver the instructions straight into your earpiece in real time. No more mistakes! What do you think?'

Shirley was still crying, but for deeply different reasons than before. 'I – I don't know what to say.'

Dave pushed her off his lap and she fell to the floor. 'Well, fucking thank-you might be a start, you ungrateful bitch!'

Dave stood up to walk out of the room before Shirley managed a, 'Thank y-'

'Too late!'

At S-Packers Tarquin was working alone this morning, and boy, did it show. He had Scissor Sister's *Take Your*

Mama booming out of a small portable stereo, he was singing along and dancing in his own super camp fashion whilst he packed.

As usual, Jerry had come through the factory to get to his office and could hear the music from outside which had been louder and louder the closer he got. He opened the door and stood there for a couple of minutes watching Tarquin dancing. He couldn't help but laugh. Jerry quietly snuck up behind Tarquin who was so engrossed in his moves that he didn't even notice, until Jerry screamed in his ear, 'You fucking bender!'

Tarquin nearly jumped out of his skin, then turned round and camply slapped Jerry on the chest. 'You fucking fat ginger twat!' As they laughed, Jerry walked over to the ghetto blaster and turned the music down. 'I'm not getting on your case or anything Tarquin but you're my responsibility and if the head honcho comes down here and sees and hears what I've just seen and heard, it'll be *my* bollocks he wants for breakfast.'

'Sounds lovely,' said Tarquin, but realising that it probably wasn't a good idea to agitate Jerry any further he added, 'OK, sorry. Are we going for a pint after work?'

Jerry mimicked Tarquin's dance moves whilst he quipped, 'As long as you've got all this faggoty dancing out of your system.' Secretly he'd decided a couple of those moves looked pretty good. He thought he might even

64

try them next time they went to a club. He scanned the room looking for Rizwan and asked, 'Where's the Asian Caucasian?'

'He's going to be late. He's got that advanced driver thingy. He told me to remind you about the lottery money.'

'Don't worry, I'll not forget. But you lot have got to make me put them on this week. You know what we're like once we get arseholed. We were lucky that no numbers came up last week and luck runs out. Fast'

'I will, and don't worry about it. There was never any chance of them being pulled out two weeks on the bounce. So we are off out again tonight then?'

'It's Friday, course we're off out.'

'Will Clive be coming?'

Tarquin's fixation with Clive amused Jerry no end. He thought that at least if Tarquin was concentrating his efforts on bending Clive he wouldn't need to try it on with him. Jerry needn't have been worried though. Tarquin had absolutely no interest in him at all. Or Rizwan for that matter. 'I don't think so,' said Jerry, 'his mum's ill or something, he rung me last night to say he wouldn't be coming in. I'll call round for him after work and see if she's any better.'

Tarquin jumped up and down, giddy with excitement. 'I'll go. Peoples' mums love me!'

Jerry reminded Tarquin of the previous faggoty dancing warning, said his goodbyes and wondered off to his office.

Rizwan sat waiting in his car for the instructor to turn up and wondered what, after ten years of driving, he could possibly be taught that he didn't already know. He looked at his watch, it was ten to nine and he hoped the instructor would be punctual.

Brian, for the first time in his life, looked like he may be running late. He'd spent that long polishing his freshly bought, nearly new one point eight Mondeo, that he'd completely lost track of time. Perhaps a lesser man would have driven a little over the speed limit to get to his destination on time, but not Brian. He stuck to the rules. He looked at his watch. Ten minutes to go, his sat nav said nine. He might just make it.

Thanks to a lucky run of green lights and the lollipop lady's insistence on a cigarette break, his nine year streak of punctuality remained intact. As Brian approached Riz's Volvo, he couldn't help but chuckle to himself smugly. Rizwan couldn't help but chuckle from simply looking at Brian. He was carrying a clipboard, wearing a pair of half mast green Farrah trousers which had a massive bulge in the right pocket, white socks, a pink Le Shark polo shirt and he was sporting the thickest jam-jar-bottom glasses Riz had ever seen. Brian knocked on the driver's side window and Riz rolled it down.

'Hi, I'm Rizwan. You must be Brian.' Riz reached his arm out of the window to shake Brian's hand. Brian snubbed the gesture and said, 'I need to take a look around the inside first, could you pop the bonnet please.' Rizwan had to try hard not to laugh, Brian had the strongest Rochdale accent he'd ever heard, he pronounced look 'luke', and around 'arewnd'.

Riz pulled a large red lever concealed under his steering wheel and the bonnet popped open. Brian walked around the back of the car to get to it which confused Rizwan.

As Brian approached the open bonnet, he couldn't help but feel impressed with how expertly he'd checked the tyres, Rizwan hadn't even noticed. He nosed around under the bonnet, checking the oil and the water. Much to his disappointment everything was fine. He closed it and asked Riz to turn on the lights and each indicator before walking round the back and asking him to press the brake pedal. Again, everything was in good working order.

Brian was damned if he was going to let this good-for-nothing drink driver get a clean sheet for the first part of the test whilst he was in charge. Relief rushed over him as he realised he hadn't yet checked the wiper blades. Everybody always got marked down for those. He got in the car and sat down in the passenger seat, rested his clipboard on the dash and removed a rear view mirror, complete with a suction pad, from his pocket. He stuck this to the windscreen in front of him and adjusted it before asking Riz to try the screen wash. To Brian's horror the wiper blades effortlessly removed every trace of the liquid, leaving the glass immaculately clean and smear free. He'd only known Rizwan for a matter of minutes and already he despised him.

Brian put on his seatbelt, 'Now, start the car and drive as you would normally drive, and remember, I'm not here to hinder you, I'm here to help you.' he lied.

Riz put his seatbelt on, much to Brian's annoyance, and started the engine.

'I'm going to take you through a series of exercises designed to improve and sharpen your inferior driving skills. I'm not here to change the world, just try and make a positive difference to the way you observe and drive. You can set off now. Just follow the road ahead at all times, unless me or the markings dictate otherwise.'

Riz carefully checked his mirrors, indicated and began to drive. Brian instructed him to take a left at the T-Junction ahead and continue on to the dual carriageway, which he once again executed perfectly before Brian said, 'Looking to the left – danger ... looking to the right – danger, always looking for danger, look,' he pointed at a bridge up ahead; Riz was trying not to laugh at his accent, the look 'luke' thing would never get boring, he decided that this may not be so bad after all. At least he'd have something funny to tell the lads in the pub later. 'What do you see?'

Riz looked confused and answered, 'A bridge?'

'That's right,' agreed Brian. 'Always looking for danger.'

Riz chuckled quietly and said, 'A bridge isn't dangerous,' before being interrupted by a clearly irate Brian, 'Well, this is where you learn your first lesson, sonny Jim, let me enlighten you. Two weeks ago in Wigan, a young illegal immigrant like yourself climbed up onto one of those there bridges and threw himself off. Landed in front of a transit van. Caused a ten car pile-up. Always. Looking. For danger.'

Rizwan was beginning to think this guy was a first class freak; illegal fucking immigrant? Rizwan had a British passport for Christ's sake! They approached some traffic lights and he came to a stop behind a red Ford Transit van.

'Whoa, whoa, whoa! More paint, more danger!' screamed Brian.

Riz, taken aback by his reaction, snapped, 'What?'

'More paint, more danger! The more paint you can see of the car in front, the more danger you're putting us in! You're far too close; all you can see is the back of that van. Imagine the catastrophe . . . you pull right up to the back of a van like this and it breaks down, let's assume the person behind you hasn't had the pleasure of my company and is as incompetent as you are, as is the person behind him and so on and so forth! You're stuck. Are you willing to take that chance? Always looking for danger. Go left at these lights into the B&Q car park and find what you consider to be a safe place to park.'

That had put Brian in a slightly better mood. Perhaps Riz had just got off to a lucky start. Everyone messed up with the B&Q car park and Brian silently prayed that Rizwan would be no exception.

As Riz reverse-parked next to a silver VW Golf, Brian's prayers were answered. The car came to a halt and Rizwan put on the handbrake. Brian was slowly shaking his head and tutting.

'Now, on reflection, what do you think was wrong with parking here?' Riz didn't know, he thought he'd parked perfectly. He looked around and said, 'Erm, am I too far from the entrance?'

Brian shook his head and answered, 'No. Take a look through your right hand window and tell me what you see.' Riz looked across at the car next to him and said, 'A Golf?'

'Not the car! The wing mirror, the wing mirror!' Riz examined the wing mirror and said, 'Oh yeah. It's scuffed.'

Brian slouched smugly and said, 'Yes. They're clearly incompetent.'

He was really starting to piss Rizwan off. 'That's a bit unfair Brian. What if they were just parked somewhere and someone else clipped their wing mirror?'

'Are you willing to take that chance?' he snapped back, 'Also, this car park is on a hill. Now, let's say someone else has parked up there and just left their trolley behind. Before you know it, that trolley's firing down this car park at high speeds and BANG! straight into your vehicle. Always looking for danger. I think the best thing would be for me to drive for a few minutes and impart some wisdom. This is your lucky day, sunshine. You're going to get to see a master at work.'

Brian got out of the car and walked around, opening Riz's door. Riz got out and went to take his seat in the passenger side. As Brian got in the car and sat down, he looked at Riz and said, 'The driving position in this car's not half as good as in the Mondeo.'

He reached under the seat, lifted up a small lever and pulled himself closer to the steering wheel. Whilst doing so he asked, 'Is this car a one point six?'

'Yeah.'

Brian smiled and said self-righteously, 'I thought so.'

He shuffled around in his chair for a moment, looked down to his left and then his right, 'Does this seat go up and down as well as forward and back?'

'No.'

'My one point eight Mondeo does.'

He started to adjust the height of the steering and asked, 'Does this go in and out as well as up and down?'

Riz shook his head.

'Mine does.'

CHAPTER SEVEN

FRIDAY 15th June – 11 a.m.

The boys felt hungry, it seemed like ages since they'd last been fed. Billy was complaining but his brother was reassuring him that the food would turn up eventually. They didn't even have the energy to muster a game of 'I don't spy', never mind 'hide and seek'. They heard something, the snap of a light switch in the distance. They could just see the light from under the door and the stairs leading up to it were now slightly illuminated. 'Told you,' said Bobby, 'this'll be our food now.' They heard the door at the top unlock, the handle turned and it opened. They weren't used to the brightness and it dazzled them, they turned their heads away, their vision blurred. They rubbed their stinging eyes and by the time they were able to focus, the door had closed. Two plates had been set down on the top step, each holding two slices of buttered toast. Bobby scrambled up the stairs and Billy hopped along behind him. They sat on the top step wolfing their breakfast down.

As they did, an eye appeared at the keyhole in the door and loud voice boomed, 'I've got my eye on you!'

Jimbob woke up and realised it was Friday; part of him wished he'd never wake up again. The five hundred pounds he'd given to Maz, the owner of the Chameleon nightclub, had merely bought him another week without a serious beating. He needed more money and fast. He couldn't sell the car because it was on hire purchase and he couldn't sell his bass or amp because they had the battle of the bands competition the following week. Fingers crossed, that could be his ticket out of the grubby world of dealing he'd managed to get himself caught up in. He'd considered just confessing all to Martin and Steve but they'd never forgive him for being so careless with his stash. He was on his own. He'd managed to scrape an extra hundred pounds together by selling some stuff to non-regulars at higher price than usual, but he was definitely pushing his luck doing that. He knew the only safe way to deal, if there was a safe way, was to people he knew, or friends of a friend. This shouldn't have included dealing to himself. Whatever he consumed still had to be paid for.

Jimbob decided it was best to just push it out of his

mind until tonight and try to talk his way into getting another week's grace. He would need to catch Maz early on in the evening though; there are people who shouldn't drink because alcohol makes them violent, there are people who shouldn't take pills because they end up doing stupid, random shit that can get them into trouble and there are people who shouldn't take cocaine because it turns them into paranoid psychopaths. Maz fell neatly into all three of these categories. At least if Jimbob caught him early on, he'd only have the cocaine to deal with.

Maz was a particularly bad person, he was a gangster and he could easily have somebody wiped out, but when you were on his good side he was a powerful ally. Appearances were everything to Maz; flash car, flash clothes, his nightclub left a little to be desired but he meant business. Jimbob thought that perhaps when the band were interviewed on the radio later on, he could squeeze in some sort of plug for the club. That might just sweeten Maz up a touch, anything would be worth a try.

As the test drew to a close, Riz was just about ready to smash Brian's face through the windscreen. He'd stopped the car and Brian was frantically flicking through his notes.

'Hurry up please, Brian, I'm supposed to be at work at half eleven.'

Brian rested the paperwork on his lap and said, 'Nearly done, remember you got yourself into this. There's no excuse for drink driving, none! Do you think I got where I am today by drink driving?'

Riz looked at Brian, refrained from punching him so hard that he landed back on his own fucking side of the Pennines and said, 'How many more times do I have to tell you people? I was spiked.'

Brian was furious. He'd checked and double checked the paperwork, he'd counted the scores three times and Rizwan had definitely passed. He broke the news to Riz who was extremely pleased that this would be the last time he'd have to share a car with such a freak and then Brian said, 'Just one more thing. Take a look through your window and tell me what you see.'

Riz saw nothing out of the ordinary, was this a final test? He scanned around and wondered what he might see if he was looking in Brian vision, maybe those stupid glasses gave him special powers. At a loss he asked, 'Danger?'

'No,' replied Brian pointing out of the drivers side window, 'That, is my one point eight Mondeo.'

Dave could see Paul pulling hard on the pub door struggling to open it and wondered what could have happened to make a grown man want to spend all his time in his night clothes talking to a toy bear. He knew Paul made some of the less regular punters feel uneasy, but, a customer was a customer, even if they were a complete loony. He went to the front doors opened them, and said, 'How may more times, Paul? It's a push door.'

Dave walked back behind the bar and Paul followed, mumbling to himself. 'Do you want the usual Paul?' He nodded and Dave walked to the fridges at the far end of the bar.

As Paul waited patiently for his drink, the bear turned to look at him and said, 'Don't forget mine.' Paul shouted over to Dave, 'And one for Theodore please.' Dave shook his head as he prepared the drinks and once he'd finished, placed them both on the bar. A small shot glass full of milk and a pint of turbo shandy; half Smirnoff Ice and half Stella.

'Two pounds eighty, please.' Paul went into his dressing gown pocket and pulled out a five pound note which he threw onto the bar. He waited patiently whilst Dave rung the order through the till and got his change. He took it from Dave popped it in his pocket, then picked up the drinks and went to sit down in the corner. That was his spot. Dave had told him off before for wandering around and upsetting the customers but he didn't mind too much as long as he stayed out of the way.

He put both the drinks down and sat the bear next to him on the fixed seating. Paul hadn't always been that way, it had been a tragedy, a tragedy that the only other two people who actually knew the ins and outs of it would rather forget. It seemed, amongst the locals in the pub, there was a new theory each week as to how Paul ended up in his condition, but nobody really knew for sure. Perhaps if they could hear the bear speak like Paul could, things might be different.

As a child, he and that bear had been inseparable. It was given to him on his fourth birthday by his mother. It was she who had given the toy its name, Theodore. He'd treasured it ever since. Although it wasn't until after she'd passed away that he became fixated with it.

Paul liked coming in to *The Nobody* when it had just opened, as it was always dead until tea time. Dave preferred it too; Paul couldn't irritate anybody if he was alone. This was benefit day though, so he would probably be in for the duration. Paul looked down at Theodore and then across at the table before asking, 'Why do I always get the milk?'

CHAPTER EIGHT

FRIDAY 15th June – 4 p.m.

'You're listening to Yorkshire's finest Y.F.F.M! Our special guests coming up next are one of two bands representing our county in the national battle of the bands competition in Manchester next Friday night. So before we speak to the lads, let's have a listen to their music. This is Jimbob Rifkin with *Steal this Song*.

The song kicked in and the three of them sat there nervously. Not good nerves though, not the kind that explode into magical adrenaline when you start playing. Bad nerves, the kind that try to eat away at your soul. The studio was smaller than they'd expected. DJ Jay was sat just across from them behind a desk with a couple of decks, a PC and a load of flashing lights. They were sat facing him at a small table with a couple of microphones popping out of the middle of it.

'OK, lads,' said Jay, 'just relax and enjoy it. I'm not asking any taxing questions, just a few daft ones texted in by the listeners and a chance for you to plug the gig. It'll be a piece of cake.'

'Yeah, cool,' said Martin, 'How long are we on for?'

'Just a couple of minutes, it's all pretty standard stuff. Just make sure you all keep the same distance from the mikes so as you're all the same volume and try not to talk over each other.'

He'd done a good job of chilling them out a little bit, as they'd originally thought the interview would be pre-recorded and weren't prepared to go out live. Martin wished they'd given them the questions beforehand so they could come up with some good answers. Steve was usually pretty good off the cuff and Jimbob was funny without meaning to be, but Martin liked to be prepared, and wasn't.

'OK, lads, one minute to go. I'll start off by asking you to introduce yourselves and what you do, that should break the ice a bit before I start on the questions. You ready?'

They were impressed. DJ Jay was a lot less of a twat in real life than he sounded on the radio, 'Ready as we'll ever be,' said Steve.

As the song came to a close, they all rehearsed over in their heads what they'd say to introduce themselves. Nothing came.

'There it was, folks, Jimbob Rifkin with *Steal this Song*

and I've got the guys sat in front of me here. Tell us a bit about each of you.'

Martin was at a blank but he wasn't going to let Steve jump in first. 'I'm Martin, I play guitar and sing. I also write everything.'

The bastard! thought Steve, we all have a hand in making those songs sound as good as they do. He might build the skeleton, but he and Jimbob made the muscle and flesh. He concealed his anger. 'I'm Steve. Drummer. One half of the rhythm section, keeping them tight!'

Keeping them tight? Jimbob held the fucking rhythm together, he realised there'd been a short silence. 'I'm James, or Jimbob! And I look after the bass! In yer face!'

Thank God Jimbob had attempted to say something slightly amusing, it had looked like it was going seriously pear-shaped for a moment.

'OK, guys, we've had our listeners text in some ques- tions and I'll fire the first one at you, Martin. What would you do if the world was going to end in five minutes?'

That wasn't music-related! What the fuck was he going to answer to that? He had to think fast, 'erm . . .' he began, 'er . . . go somewhere else?'

DJ Jay started to laugh, as did Steve and Jimbob. He'd pulled it off. He was relieved at his unconscious wit and sat back knowing he could relax whilst the other two dealt with a question each.

'Now here's one for you, Jimbob. What's the most rock and roll thing you've ever done?'

Jesus Christ! Where did he start? None of the stuff they'd got up to was suitable for broadcasting across the whole of Yorkshire. He was dying to say armed robbery but managed to bite his tongue, 'I once put a teabag in a cup and poured hot water on it!'

'Good answer,' said Jay. 'You guys are really living life on the edge. So Steve, what are your influences and if you had to describe your music in three words, what would they be?'

Quick as a flash Steve replied, 'Saturday Night Fever, Keith and Orville, The Jackson Five and general funkiness.'

'And your music in three words.'

'I. Don't. Know.'

They were off to a flying start, the nerves had all but disappeared and they comfortably breezed through the rest of the interview. Jimbob even managed to get a plug in for the club.

The last half hour of Friday at S-Packers had to be Jerry's least favourite time of day as it dragged no end. He'd polished off everything he had to do by three and just bided his time until he could clock off and get to the boozer. He decided to look for some porn on the internet to pass the time a little quicker. He went to Google and stroked his chin thoughtfully for a moment before typing in 'black bird's tits'. He chuckled to himself at the results; he meant black-bird's tits not fucking blackbirds and blue tits. He clicked the back button and pondered again for a moment as to what to put in. Then, out of sheer curiosity rather than a desire to actually visit the sites that came up, he typed in 'fat porn chicken'. He was surprised at the results.

He clicked the back button again and decided to get down to searching for something worth looking at. 'Nude naked xxx tits boobs fanny minge stockings,' that ought to do it. He visited the first site on the list and sat stroking his cock whilst he admired the stocking-ed legs of a tasty brunette. He had a bit of an unhealthy weakness for stockings.

CHAPTER NINE

FRIDAY 15th June – 6 p.m.

Tarquin approached Clive's front door determined to get him out of the house and over to the pub. He knocked loudly and waited. Inside, Clive had just finished washing his mother and had lifted her from the wheelchair into her armchair in front of the television. He put BBC on; she liked to watch the news, and went to open the door.

As he did so, an overwhelming stench hit Tarquin's face with a fierce force, like heat escaping when an oven door has been opened too quickly.

'Fucking hell, Clive. What's that smell? It's disgusting.'

'Sssshh, you'll upset her, it's my mum she's not well and she had a bit of an accident. I've had to bath her.'

Tarquin felt physically sick. Not just at the smell but at the thought of Clive having to wash his own mother's arse. 'Well, I just came to see if you were coming for a pint with us?'

'I can't, my mum's not well. I've told you.'

Tarquin barged past Clive and headed towards the living room door saying, 'I'll have a word with her.' Clive quickly headed after him and pulled him back. 'No. She's funny with people. I'll have a word with her.' He walked Tarquin back to the door and added, 'To be honest I could actually do with a few pints. I'm knackered. You set off. I'll talk her round, get a shower and catch up with you in a bit.'

Jonny T. arrived home from a tough day's work selling cars; he was eating a Pot Noodle he'd just bought from the petrol station on the way home. He plonked himself down in front of the TV and picked up the Gazette to have a flick through, it was free ads day and he reckoned he might be able to pick up a couple of bargain motors over the weekend. He'd had a few really good weeks. Brian had helped, he ended up paying way over the odds for that cut and shut Mondeo. On the front page there was a story about a gas man that had gone missing, this village was like a black hole. People went missing all the time.

His concentration didn't last long before he started to feel sorry for himself. His affliction was a burden. All he wanted was the love of a good woman. Sitting there feeling lonely, he sighed and began to cry. He hadn't realised that his mum had decided not to go to bingo. She heard him from the kitchen and came rushing in.

'What's up, Jonny love? Why the glum face? Is business not going so well?'

Jonny looked up all squelchy-eyed and replied, 'Business is *shit, knacker*, fine.' The fact he hadn't even managed to get through such a simple sentence upset him even more and he cried harder. His mum came over and knelt beside him. She placed a comforting hand on his knee and said, 'Come on, love. It can't be so bad. You can tell me. What's wrong, love? I might be able to help?'

Jonny wiped his running nose with the back of his hand and said, 'Do you think I'll ever be able to find someone, mum? I'm thirty years old and I've never had a *fuck, shag*, girlfriend.'

His mum pulled her sleeve forward over her hand and wiped away Jonny's remaining snot and tears. 'Of course you will, love,' she said comfortingly, 'but not while you're sat in here crying into your Pot Noodle. You need to get out and meet people. Play the field, you never know, you might score.'

She reached across him and grabbed the *Gazette*, flicked through and ripped out a page. 'Look, what about this?' she passed it to him. 'The lonely hearts page. We could put you an advert in there.'

'Who'd want to go out with me? They all just laugh

when I, *knacker, twat*, start swearing.' He screwed the page up and threw it on the floor.

'Don't be so negative. You've done amazingly well with your affliction, sure you still swear quite a bit but you don't tick and twitch anymore. We'll put you an ad in, they can't hear you swearing in an advert. You can go out and meet them and if they don't like you, so what! You never have to see them again, and at least it'll get you out and about.'

Tarquin had just rolled another pound into the fruit machine. Riz and Jerry stood watching and barking orders at him on how to play. Jerry was the main offender. 'If you pack fudge as shite as you play bandits, it's a wonder S-Packers hasn't gone fucking bust.'

Tarquin glanced around just long enough to throw some daggers eyes. 'I'm pretty good at packing fudge. Actually.'

'I bet you are, you gay bastard,' said Jerry as he tried moving him out of the way. 'Shift over, let me show you how to drop the jackpot.' Neither of them let him. Jerry had a bit of a problem with gambling, mainly in that he never won. Ever. Even when he did win he kept piling in the pounds until he'd lost. Tarquin was beginning to regret having a flutter now.

Riz tried to change the subject and get them both away

from the flashing lights saying to Tarquin, 'Weren't you supposed to be going to get Clive?'

'That's a good point,' Jerry intervened. 'Where is he?' he nudged Tarquin in the back. 'You said you were off to go get him.'

'I did, he wanted to get a shower first. He's on his way.' He finished his last spin of the bandit wheels and beckoned them to follow him to a table. 'Here, his mum had shit herself today and Clive had had to bath her. How disgusting is that.'

Jerry couldn't help laughing. 'Just you wait until he gets here,' he said, 'I'll give him some right grief.' Rizwan as usual jumped to Clive's defence. 'No you fucking won't, you fat bastard. Leave him alone.' Jerry tended to listen when he got called fat. It really pissed him off. He wasn't that big. Not anymore.

'Ssssshhhh he's here,' Tarquin whispered. As Clive approached the table, Jerry was trying hard not to laugh. He had to do something fast, and much as he was going to regret it, the first thing to come out of his mouth was, 'Can I get you a pint?' Bastard. Of all the things to say. Jerry had let himself down, and surprised everyone else in the process. The professional round dodger had just actually volunteered out of turn to go to the bar.

This was too good an opportunity to miss for Riz and Tarquin who both said, 'Yeah. Go on then.'

'Erm . . . I meant Clive, not you two,' said Jerry.

'Come on you tight bastard,' said Rizwan, 'I'll have a glass of Jack and Coke.'

'You'll have a glass of shut the fuck up! What do you think I am, made of money?'

'You get paid more than us! I'll just have a pint then.'

Jerry walked off to the bar in a huff; at least he didn't feel like laughing anymore. Over at the table, the other two were warning Clive not to let Jerry near the fruit machine. He came back with the drinks and said, 'Look, that fucking loony's over there in the corner. Getting pissed at the tax payer's expense.'

Clive sprung to life, he actually had something interesting to say for once. 'I heard a rumour that he went mad because he used to work at a place testing drugs on animals and he started testing them on himself. It sent him nuts apparently and they bought him that bear so he could do mad experiments on that instead.'

Jerry, blunt as ever, said, 'All I know is, he's a fucked up bastard.'

Tarquin excused himself and headed off to the loo, winking at Clive on the way past. Clive almost choked on his drink.

CHAPTER TEN

FRIDAY 15th June – 9 p.m.

Dave was in his office staring at the seven monitors which covered every inch of the pub and its premises, in front of it was a console with all manner of lights, sticks and dials on it. Concentrating his efforts on 'Monitor 1 – Exterior Left', he wished it was within his budget to employ a car park attendant so that the cars could be organised according to type and colour. He considered just unplugging the camera to save his discomfort but decided against it. It would only give Shirley an excuse to make mistakes.

He switched his attention to 'Monitor 4 – Restaurant Right' and spotted something. He grabbed his joystick and carefully panned the camera slightly before zooming in. Then he pressed a button on the console and said, 'Table two needs an ashtray, and there's a beer mat short on three.' From the monitor next to it he could see Shirley standing behind the bar. She looked straight into the camera and stuck up her thumb to let Dave know she'd heard him before promptly sorting the problem out. As he watched her marching to his tune, Dave slouched into his chair, pleased with himself. He knew those cameras would be a good idea.

Back downstairs, Jerry had just rolled his fifteenth pound into the fruit machine. The rest had given up hope of getting him off it this evening and were just stood around watching him lose.

'Fucker! There's a two on there and if it holds we'll get a bonus. It's ready to drop. Who's got another fucking quid?' Jerry looked around expecting them to pass one over but nobody obliged.

'Come on! It's ready, it'll pay out now I'm telling you!'

Rizwan opened his empty pockets, 'Look, Jerry, the only money I've got left is the lottery money in my back pocket which I confiscated from you earlier.'

Jerry reached out his upturned hand and waved his fingers back and forth as if using an invisible toilet room soap dispenser. 'Well, crack it out then you tight bastard!'

'I can't. This'll be two weeks in a row. Don't involve me in you pissing it up the wall. We're proper pushing our luck.'

'Come on, just a tenner, I'll put it back out of the winnings. It's going to drop. I'm telling you.'

Jerry continued piling cash into the fruit machine for another couple of hours before asking again, 'Come on just a tenner, I'll put it back out of the winnings. It's going to drop. I'm telling you.'

'It's all gone, Jerry, you've fucking spent it all.'

'BASTARD! Drive to the cash point for us, Riz.'

Rizwan's reply was simple. 'You can bollocks.' Then, to soften the blow he said, 'Tell you what, I will drive to a cash point, but we're not coming back here. We'll go out to a club and pull some birds. Like you said last week.'

Jerry took a lingering look at the hypnotic lights of the fruit machine and then weighed it up in his mind against the possibility of getting a shag later on. 'OK then,' he said, 'let's go.'

CHAPTER ELEVEN

FRIDAY 15th June – 11 p.m.

Holme Bridge's attempt at a nightclub was a particularly strange example. Chameleon looked more like a youth club with ashtrays. It opened until five thirty and was a bit of a mismatch. Every night was Karaoke night but it was mingled in amongst banging house tunes or old party classics. That didn't matter though, because whatever Chameleon disguised itself as, it was still shite. Its clientèle was made up of the dregs of the village, out of town hardcore pill heads and anybody too young to get served anywhere else.

Tarquin had decided not to join them; evidently pulling birds wasn't his thing. Jerry was obviously looking at women through beer-tinted shades, because he was hard at work on chatting up the big fat ugly 'un he'd had the piss taken out of him for shagging only the week before. It was turning Clive and Rizwan's stomach to watch, so when they heard him say to her, 'You smell of chips . . . have you got any?' they decided it was time to leave him to it and made their way to the dance floor. You had to hand it to Jerry though, he was one smooth talker. 'So,' he asked, 'do you take it up the arse?' The music was so loud she hadn't heard him properly, so she just laughed. Jerry wished she'd stop fucking laughing and just answer the question.

He had a two drink rule. If you've not got commitment from a bird that there's a guaranteed shag by the time you've bought her two drinks, she's clearly just a tight bitch who's not interested in sex. She's obviously only interested in scamming drinks out of unsuspecting blokes, but Jerry was too smart for that. She was half way down her second Archers and lemonade and it was time for him to get some clarification on the situation. 'So,' he paused for a moment whilst he tried to remember her name. 'Janet.' She'd not corrected him, bonus, he must have got it right. 'Do you fancy coming back to mine for a fuck?'

Again, she'd not heard him correctly through the music. 'Excuse me?'

Jerry leaned over and shouted in her ear, 'I said! Do you fancy coming back to mine! For. A. Fuck!'

How rude, she couldn't believe he was being so for-ward. He wasn't like this last time they'd got together. 'No! No I don't, you filthy pig!'

She was right, he thought, his place was a little bit untidy. 'All right, all right. Calm down, Jeanette,' he said, grabbing her huge arse. 'We'll go to your place then.'

She forcefully removed his hand. 'My name is Janine!'

Jerry was losing patience, 'All right. Do you fancy a fuck, *Janine*? Jesus!'

'Not with you I don't.'

Tight-arsed drink-scamming bitch! It was time for Jerry to turn on the charm. 'Come on, love. Look at it this way. We both know what's going to happen. We can do one of two things. I can buy you a drink, you can buy me a drink, we can have a dance then a couple more drinks and then we'll end up going home together and shagging. *Or*, we can skip that bit out and just go back to mine *or yours* and have a shag now.'

Meanwhile in the upstairs office Jimbob was about to try and talk his way out of a serious pasting. Maz was sat at his desk with a small mound of coke in front of him. He was no Scarface; it was only a couple of grams. He dipped his head to snort a line and Jimbob stood nervously waiting to be asked the question he'd been dreading hearing. Maz finished his line, sat back, pulled his nose up like he was doing a pig impression, sniffed up aggressively and looked Jimbob straight in the eyes. He was a scary-looking mother fucker. Built like a brick shithouse, he was Pakistani, or maybe Indian, but he shaved off his hair so people thought he was black. He even spoke with a mock Jamaican accent. 'So, Jim Man, you got me fucking money?'

Jimbob cleared his throat and pulled out the hundred

pounds he'd managed to skank from his pocket. He placed it on the table and said, 'I've got a ton there for you. The rest's on its way, I just need a bit more time.'

Maz leaned over and counted the money; he took a Marlboro Light from his packet and lit it. He took a long, deep drag and blew the smoke at Jimbob. 'Hundred's no good enough, man. I fucking told you last week. It is time to pay up. You should know better. Never get high off your own supply.'

'Listen, Maz,' said Jimbob, struggling to keep his cool, 'I'll get it. You know I'll get it. I know I fucked up but I'm trying my best here to sort it out, mate. I've not taken anything from the stash you've been selling me for weeks and I'm chipping away at the debt.'

'I'm getting a bit fucking fed up with your excuses, Jimmy boy!' Maz stood up and took another drag of his cigarette. Jimbob had to think fast.

'Look, Maz, did you hear the radio earlier? Have you noticed how much busier it is tonight?'

'No, I didn't hear. But yes, I have noticed.'

'I plugged the club earlier on Y.F.F.M. Ask anyone. I was on the air with the band and I advertised the club. It'd have cost you hundreds to get exposure like that.' Jimbob prayed this could buy him some time.

'You mentioned the club?' Maz took his seat again.

'Yeah, man. I don't expect you to knock any of my

debt off or anything, just give us a bit more time. You know I'm good for it. Maz, I'm sorry, I really am, but the important thing is you can trust me. Even though I've made a mistake you know I'll never fuck you over and I do a good job in here. You know I do.'

Maz snorted another long line of coke, sat up wiped his nose and said, 'I'll give you two fucking weeks! I appreciate the work you do for me, man, but if you let me down again, I'll fuck you up. You have to understand that I can't be seen letting shit like this slide, it compromises me position of power. I'm sorry, Jimbob, but for every hundred quid you come in short, I'm going to have to break a fucking finger or a toe, man. This is nothing personal. Just business.'

Jimbob had had a lucky escape. He shook Maz's hand and left the room and he immediately had to run to the toilet to vomit. Whilst he hung his head over the seat, coughing and struggling to catch his breath, he realised he was going to have to come up with something quickly. A nice big fat juicy line would sort him out a treat but inevitably would only add to his problem. He was lucky to get two weeks, but his schedule with the band left him little time to get a plan together. He knew he couldn't do anything until after the competition had been and gone next week. He got up from the toilet and took a mouthful of tap water; he swished it around his mouth and spat it into the sink before washing his hands and heading off downstairs to get on with his job.

Downstairs on the dance floor Rizwan was feeling a little bit uncomfortable. It looked like Clive had managed to pull a girl that wouldn't even appear on Jerry's radar. He decided to go over and try and prevent him making a fool of himself. 'Hi, excuse me, love, can I just borrow my mate for a second?'

She looked up at him and said, 'Yeah, sure.'

Clive set off walking towards the bar with Riz, he turned back round and shouted over to the girl, 'I'll be back in a minute!' Then he turned to Riz and asked, 'What the fuck are you doing? I was enjoying myself there.'

Rizwan grabbed his arm and pulled him along to the bar. 'I was saving you making from a twat of yourself. You'd have regretted that in the morning.'

Clive was upset that Rizwan had chosen to interfere. 'When I want your advice I'll ask for it. Anyway, what's wrong with her?'

'Well look,' said Riz as he spun Clive around and pointed back towards the dance floor, 'she's in a fucking wheelchair for a start.'

Clive was gob-smacked. With all the prejudice Riz had had to endure in his thirty year life, he was judging someone by the way they looked. 'You should know better than to say something like that. She was sat at the side of the dance floor looking miserable so I thought I'd go over and cheer her up. It can't be that often she gets to dance.'

Riz ordered them a bottle of Stella each. 'OK, mate. Sorry. I was just looking out for you. Tell you what, I'll get her a drink and you can go back over there with it.'

Clive was pleased, but also concerned that Riz might just sneak out when he went to take the drink over. 'Thanks, Riz, she's on cider and black. You won't leave me in here, will you?'

Riz added a cider and black to the drinks order. Fucking hell, that's all he needed, he thought; hanging around in here while Clive danced with a cripple. Clive needed looking after though, and if the boot was on the other foot he'd definitely do it for Riz. 'OK, I'll stay. I'll be over here if you want me. You wanna tell that girl to be careful.'

Clive was confused. Why would she need to be careful? 'What do you mean?' he asked.

Rizwan passed him the cider and black, motioned as if he was pushing a wheelchair and said, 'Drink driving!'

Clive laughing, weaved his way back to the dance floor. She was sat there waiting for him exactly where he'd left her. He reached over and handed her the cider and black. 'There you go, Lisa.' She took the drink and said, 'Thanks. What did your mate want?'

Clive shook his head. 'Nothing much. Just to buy us a drink.' He looked over and stuck his thumb up at Riz. Lisa looked across and mouthed the words, 'thank you'. Clive was impressed by her wheelchair. It was much better than his mum's. Lisa's had a cup holder in the arm and a motor so she could get herself around easily. She also had some cool stickers on it that glowed under the club's fluorescent lights.

Clive carefully put his bottle of Stella on the floor and grabbed Lisa by the hands, dancing with her by swaying his hips and moving their arms, in much the same way as a father would dance with his toddler daughter. As the music livened up, Clive started to get ambitious and threw in a couple of side steps. He was having such a good time he didn't even notice he'd knocked his bottle over.

Riz was still stood by the bar, watching. He didn't feel as embarrassed from back there. He scanned the room to see if he could see Jerry but he must have gone home with the fat bird because he couldn't see either of them.

Riz turned his attention back to Clive who was really going for it now. Step to the left, step to the right, a little shuffle forward and a little shuffle back, all the while waving Lisa's arms from left to right. Then something happened; he saw it as if it was happening in slow motion. As Clive was shuffling back, his foot landed on the Stella bottle. It rolled under his shoe causing him to lean so far back that he started to fall over.

Clive was panicking, he could feel himself going and his instant gut reaction was to tense every muscle in his body to prevent him from falling. Unfortunately for Lisa, this included his hands which were now tightly grasping hers. As he fell backwards, he yanked her right out of the wheelchair and she landed full force on top of him.

Clive began to go to pieces. She was heavy, that wheelchair had disguised how big she actually was. He couldn't move her and she certainly couldn't move herself. He was stuck with Lisa clamped on top of him, a dead weight.

Rizwan really wanted to go and help but the people in the club who had seen this incident fell into two categories; too stunned to move, or rolling about laughing. Rizwan fell into the latter. He could barely even see Clive anymore through the tears in his eyes.

Clive needed to do something. Why wasn't anybody helping? He tried to shout but Lisa was so heavy on his chest he could barely even breathe. She was in a worse state than he was, crying and screaming. He tried to lift his left shoulder but it wasn't going anywhere. Luckily, he had a bit of leverage with his right. He lifted it sharply with all his strength and Lisa slid slightly. He repeated the process a few times until he had enough room to squeeze out. He got to his feet to see pretty much everybody in the club laughing at him, then looked down on the floor at Lisa, lying there face down crying. He didn't know what to do, so he bolted, and Rizwan charged out after him.

At Janine's place, Jerry was beginning to think he'd made a huge mistake. In the brightly lit lights of her apartment he'd realised that the lads hadn't been lying to him about her looks after all. The bastard child of an overweight Gail Tilsley from Coronation Street five years into a crystal meth addiction, and E.T. Although this bothered him, he was fucked if he wasn't going to get his cock wet after all this effort. She grabbed him by the hand and led him upstairs to the bedroom. He usually made a point of keeping his eyes open when kissing a girl. Closing your eyes was for poofs, but this time he made an exception. At least if he kept them closed, he could imagine he was copping off with someone else.

All he could think about, however, was whether or not, once he'd managed to get her in the sack, she might smell. He considered suggesting a nice romantic bath together but decided against it as this would only prolong the time he would have to spend with her. He decided if she did smell, it was just too bad, he'd have to close his nose as well as his eyes.

'Shall we set the mood a bit?' he asked. 'This light's a

bit bright.' She looked up at him and he tried not to make eye contact; he didn't want to turn to stone.

'Yeah,' she replied. 'Shall I light some candles?'

Fuck. That backfired. More lights was the last thing he wanted. He could see the moon beaming in through the skylight window and thought of an excuse fast. 'No. Just turn the lights off. Moonlight is really romantic, don't you think?'

Surprised and impressed, she obliged. That was better, he thought; the moonlight had made everything soft focus, it was much easier to manage. She proceeded to slowly take off all her clothes. She was trying to look seductive and sexy but for Jerry, it was almost vomit-inducing. His stomach turned as he saw her rolls of flab falling out. Her tits were so saggy that her nipples looked like a pair of cartoon eyes staring down at the laminate flooring.

Jerry knew that while she was doing this he'd be expected to watch and enjoy it, so he decided to take action. As she walked towards him, her alien face getting closer and closer, he decided he'd just have to shag her from behind. He wasted no time and wanted this over as fast as possible so, as she approached, he grabbed her hand, spun her around so quickly that it was almost a pirouette and bent her over.

He wasted no time in getting on with it and cracked on thinking of every edition of FHM he'd knocked one out over for the last four years. He went all the way through the one hundred sexiest women list, the high street honeys and all the centrefolds, all the time with his eyes firmly shut and his face gurning. He usually enjoyed the slapping sound he heard when he banged a girl from behind; it was like someone invisible was standing watching and clapping at his stellar performance, but this sounded like a full round of applause.

It was putting him off. He opened his eyes for long enough to see the moonlight bouncing off her more than ample arse. This illumination combined with the cellulite dimples on it actually made it look like the surface of the moon. He realised he'd now completely lost concentration and was starting to lose his erection, so he clamped his eyes tight shut again and, in an effort to get hard once more, his thoughts moved to his favourite famous female singers, then his favourite actresses. He was getting there now, it was only a matter of time. His legs were trembling and his mouth was gurning even more, the end of his ordeal was nearly upon him and as he reached the final few thrusts he let out a large growl. Then she pulled away. What the fuck did she do that for? he thought. He couldn't believe it. After all the effort and hard work he'd gone to, it didn't seem fair for her to pull away, especially on the vinegar stroke.

'I want you to cum on my face,' she said and moved

over to the bed. She lay down with her head leaning back over the edge, in a position that was supposed to be sexy. Jerry paced over and stood above her, masturbating furiously, but he'd run out of material. He had absolutely nothing left, poor Jerry had withdrawn every woman in his wank account whilst he was shagging her. He tried going back through them but it was no good, it wasn't working. He couldn't think of anybody at all. He opened his eyes to see her alien face looking up at him. There was no other option. He couldn't carry on anymore and it wasn't like he could fake it. He was going to have to be honest. He dropped his cock, sighed and said, 'Sorry, Julie. I don't think I can.'

CHAPTER TWELVE

FRIDAY 22nd June - 8 a.m.

Dave got up off the floor and picked up his screwdriver. 'Shirley!'

She quickly scurried over. 'Yes, love?'

He pointed to the fruit machine he'd been tinkering with for the last hour. 'We need a new fruit machine. I've tried my best but I can't fix it. I knew burning those manuals was a mistake. Do you see the trouble you've caused me with your pathetic, work-shy attitude!'

She tried to apologise but, as usual, Dave butted in. 'Yes, yes, sorry, again. If you were as proficient at getting the job done as you were at being sorry, we'd never be in these situations. Unfortunately, my darling, the only thing you're good at is fucking up. At my expense.'

She began to flap. He looked like he was ready to go off on one, she had to do something, 'What do you want me to do? I can make it right. I can make it right.'

Dave thought for a moment before saying, 'Do something cost effective with the old fruit machine!'

What the hell could she do with a broken fruit machine? 'What's wrong with it?'

Dave kicked it, 'It won't pay out. Nobody's been on it since last Friday. I left it as long as I could get away with it but they've wised up. It's no longer cost-effective.'

A fruit machine that won't pay out. Why couldn't he have told her yesterday? It could have been in the *Gazette* today. She decided that once she'd finished her prep, she'd get the Yellow Pages out and try to flog it. At the end of the day, whatever she did would be wrong anyway, so what did it matter?

Jerry had got to work early that morning and was busy surfing the internet looking for porn when Clive knocked on his office door. He frantically closed the web browser and opened up the operating system for S-Packers. 'Come In!'

As Clive walked through the door, Jerry could smell another sickie coming. He didn't give Clive time to even ask before he said, 'The answer is no!'

'Please, Jerry. I'm not a piss-taker, you know I'm not. But you know how poorly my mum has been and I just want to do something nice for her. She's been wanting to go to the pictures for ages.' Clive knew he was going to have to come up with something better than this for Jerry to let him leave and added, 'She won't let me go out tonight if I don't take her, and I want to ask out that Doreen from *The Nobody*.'

He had Jerry's attention now. Much as Jerry didn't want to let him go, he would enjoy watching Clive make a twat of himself by asking Doreen out later on. He decided to get a firm commitment from Clive. 'OK. You've got a deal.'

What did he mean, 'deal'? Clive never mentioned any deal. 'Eh?'

Jerry leaned back in his chair and cracked his knuckles. 'I'll let you go, if you ask Doreen out tonight!'

Clive's bluff had been called. This was it, gauntlet thrown down. He had no option. He was going to have to do it. 'OK then.'

Jerry leaned forward and smiled. 'You better do, or I'll set Tarquin on you.'

Jonny was asleep. He was having a fantastic dream about having sex with Tracey Barlow from *Coronation Street*. He didn't have Tourette's in his dreams and he enjoyed them immensely. This one ended prematurely with his mother shouting, 'It's in! It's in!' Strangely, at the time her voice pierced his dream it wasn't coming from his mother's mouth, it was coming from Tracey Barlow's, and what she'd said was absolutely correct.

He opened his eyes and struggled to focus, then he thought quickly and rolled onto his side to save his and his mother's embarrassment. His member had sprung to attention during the dream and he'd been pitching a massive tent in the duvet.

She burst through the door waving the *Gazette*. Jonny was still struggling to focus when she hit him around the head with it, yelling, 'Come on! Wakey, wakey! Those cars won't sell themselves!'

Jonny wasn't a morning person and was irritated that his dream had been cut short. 'So fucking what!' he shouted.

His mum waved the paper in front of his face. 'Come on, get motivated and get to work, your phone'll be red hot later on when all those lovely ladies see this advert!'

Jonny sat up in bed regretting that he'd let her talk him into placing the advert in the first place. 'Mum. Why would anybody want to *fuck, shag*, go on a date with me?'

She opened the paper and sat next to him reading his advert out. 'Because . . . you're a good-looking, successful business man with a G.S.O.H.'

Jonny didn't have a clue what she was on about and looked at her blankly. 'G.S.O.H.?'

'Yes, good sense of humour.'

Jonny couldn't believe it. What sort of sad bastard would put that in their ad? He knew he should have just done it himself. 'Fucking hell, mum. They'll all think I'm a right *cock, knacker, fanny,* idiot.'

She closed the paper and reassured him. 'Everyone does it, love. Stop being so glum. If I weren't your mother, I'd go for you.'

Jonny's stomach turned and his once erect penis instantly flopped. 'That's disgusting.'

Jerry had just received some news from S-Packers' head office and was on his way down to break it to Rizwan and Tarquin. They were both hard at work for a change, forming a neat two-man production line. Jerry stopped for a moment to admire their speed and organisation. He couldn't help but think it was such a pity they hadn't been so organised from the start. It would be a shame to split them up. He walked over and to get their attention he turned off the music. 'Right you two,' he interrupted, 'I've got some good news and some bad news. What do you want first?'

They stopped packing and looked at one another suspiciously. Rizwan glanced back at Jerry. 'The bad news?'

Jerry sighed and said, 'I'm sorry lads. We've lost the fudge contract. You're fudge-packing days are well and truly over.'

Tarquin jumped into the conversation aggressively and said, 'So we're fucking sacked? What's the fucking good news?' He threw the box he'd been labelling at Jerry's feet. 'We get to keep this box of fudge?'

For once, Rizwan was on Tarquin's side and added, 'We've worked our arses off for you! Neither of us skank off work like Clive does. I know I went off to court and did that driving thingy, but only because I drive you around everywhere when I've been drinking!'

Jerry had never seen them so uptight, 'There's good news, remember.'

Tarquin took a step forward. 'Well, you'd better get on with it then. We're all fucking ears!'

'We have got a couple of other vacancies. Unfortunately you can't work together anymore, but you can decide between yourselves who wants what and let me know.'

This instantly caught Rizwan's attention. Perhaps he might be able to finally break out of the warehouse and get a cushty office job upstairs. He could fancy that, strolling around in a suit and doing bugger all all day. Part of him was sad that he wouldn't be working with Tarquin. He'd grown to really like him. But not in a gay way.

Jerry continued, 'We've got one for the butcher's contract, taking the sausages through there,' he pointed towards the back door leading to the transport depot, 'or a vacancy with the football contract. All you need to do is pick each shirt up and check the numbers on the back are on straight. Let me know what you decide.'

Rizwan was extremely disappointed at these options and shouted, 'I don't fucking believe it!'

Tarquin couldn't quite grasp the severe nature of Rizwan's annoyance. 'Oh, stop being such a miserable twat, will you? At least we get to keep our jobs!' he snapped.

Rizwan turned to face Tarquin. 'It's all right for you!' he shouted. 'I've got to go from being a fudge packer to either being a shirt lifter or taking fucking meat through the back entrance!'

The boys had been discussing how close it must be to their birthday. It seemed like a year since the last one and their intuition was usually bang on, even though their track of time was severely impaired. Christmas had been cancelled a long time ago and they'd been told in no uncertain terms that Santa Claus wasn't real and Jesus never existed. They'd been discussing the best things they could ask for. Some tunnelling equipment was a popular and obvious choice. Although highly unlikely. It would be nice to perhaps read some books, if only they could see in the dark.

As they continued their discussion they heard some footsteps coming towards the door. This was an unscheduled visit! What could be happening? It wasn't feeding time. Could it be him? Would they finally get to see him? The light outside went on and they could see two dark shadows where his feet must be. They held each other tightly as the door unlocked and then opened. As usual, the light was so bright they needed to turn away. They could hear the footsteps getting closer and closer.

It took a few seconds for their eyes to adjust. As they gained focus, they realised it wasn't him. It was her, as usual.

'Well boys, it's birthday time again. Is there anything special you want this year?' asked Shirley, leaning over and smiling.

They shared a few seconds of silence before Bobby said, 'It'd be nice to be let out of here.'

Shirley agreed completely. There was nothing she wanted more than to share a normal family life with her sons and their father but it just wasn't to be. 'Now you know that's not possible. Daddy says you're bad for business. Maybe you'll be old enough next year.'

Typical! thought Billy, *always next year, how old did they need to be? They were eight this time.* But he thought fast; what could she buy that'd get him out of here fast? 'What about a shovel?'

Shirley didn't know why she'd bothered asking them. She already knew exactly what they were getting. 'I think daddy would like it if you wanted a fruit machine.'

A fruit machine? What the hell were they supposed to do with a fruit machine? Although looking on the bright side, literally, at least they'd have a bit of light.

CHAPTER THIRTEEN

FRIDAY 22nd June – 5 p.m.

As the adverts rolled on the cinema screen, one of Clive's pet hates came up to niggle at him. Why did people laugh hysterically at the adverts when they'd clearly seen them before a million times on the television at home? He bowed his head, stuck his fingers in his ears and began humming until the feature started.

Clive's mother had a strange taste in films for a fragile, wheelchair-bound old lady. *Texas Chainsaw Massacre* was a bizarre and unusual choice. They sat watching it in complete silence; she had the popcorn resting on her lap, although she didn't seem too interested in it. Clive was slurping down his Pepsi and leaning over to get handfuls which he shovelled furiously down his throat.

Who could have possibly thought that putting that ad in the gazette would have actually worked? Jonny had shut up shop early after receiving two phone calls responding to his advert. He sorted out a date for a week the following Friday with a lass called Mary and a lovely sounding girl called Janine had called; he'd arranged to meet up with her for a late lunch. There was little choice in the way of eateries in Holme Bridge, it was either *Dusk till Dawn*, a Mexican, or *Oui Oui*, a very expensive, though unfortunately named, French restaurant. Jonny wasn't overly keen on Mexican because everything on the menu was more or less exactly the same. That left him with only one option. So what if everything on the menu was in French and he wouldn't be able to understand a word of it? So what if it was nearly ten quid for a starter? This was his first ever date and he'd been looking for an excuse to eat here ever since it opened.

He was dressed to impress. He had chosen his blue pin-stripe suit and had complemented it with a pink shirt and tie. He thought the suit represented the shrewd and successful business man in him whilst the shirt and tie reflected his softer, less threatening side. He was praying his Tourette's wouldn't put her off, but had decided that, if all else failed, this would definitely be a good lesson in self control for him. He thought that if he went on enough dates and got enough practice, he might conquer his affliction once and for all.

She had told him she'd be wearing a red blouse and would put a copy of the Gazette on the table so he could recognise her. He approached the restaurant and took a second to check his reflection in the glass on the entrance door. He was impressed. He opened it and walked inside, carefully scanning the room for Janine, and then he saw her. Fucking hell. He prayed he was mistaken. He was surprised she'd not said she'd leave an anal probe on the table instead of a Gazette. He hoped she had a mobile because this bitch needed to fucking phone home.

Janine wondered if this could be him. She was confused how somebody so drop-dead gorgeous could need to put an advert in the paper. He was well-dressed, well-groomed and clearly had a bob or two. She prayed that he wasn't like that wanker from the week before. She couldn't believe she'd slept with him. Again. As he began to walk over she could feel herself blushing.

Jimbob Rifkin were backstage, they were slap bang in the middle of the running order, exactly where they hoped they'd be. Not so early as everyone would be sober and not so late as everyone would be too pissed to be taking any notice.

The backstage area was plush. They were used to getting changed in the staff toilets but this was nice. They could get used to this. It comprised of two rooms; a ten foot square sitting area with two leather couches, and a table. The back wall was one huge mirror and the opposite wall was furnished with autographed pictures of some of the more famous bands that had played there. Primal Scream, Shed Seven and even Oasis. It didn't do a great deal for their nerves, though. The other room was a large en-suite; strangely, this was where the fridge was.

This was just one of about ten rooms but they couldn't imagine any of the other bands having a better one. They even had their name on a plaque on the door.

It had been the first time they'd been given the opportunity of having a rider list and they didn't want to come across like a bunch of prima donnas. They simply asked for some water and some Budweiser. So there they were, nervous and excited, with a few hours wait ahead of them, a fridge full of beer and a belly full of butterflies. They'd made a pact that they wouldn't drink or take any drugs until after their performance. It was too important. The two thousand strong crowd that awaited them once they hit the stage was a far cry from the tiny gaggle of no-notice-taking punters they were used to playing in front of at *The Nobody* every other month.

Jonny slowly approached the table wondering why the girl's face was going so red. Was she going to explode? He rehearsed his greeting in his mind over and over and was just about to speak when she broke the silence. 'Hi, I'm Janine, you must be Jonny.' That had thrown him off track, he reached out, shook her hand and said, 'Yes, *fat cunt*!'

Bollocks! He'd not even managed to get through his opening sentence and he'd already messed it up.

'What?' asked Janine.

He needed to think fast, make it right. 'I said, did you have far to come?' His voice lifted slightly at the end like a salesman pitching a price that was way too high and he hoped he had managed to get away with his lie.

'Oh!' Janine giggled, she couldn't believe she'd misheard him. 'No. I just live around the corner.'

Phew, thought Jonny as he took his seat across from her. He decided he'd wait for her to speak. He glanced at the Gazette. Another missing persons case on the front page, as usual.

Janine was uncomfortable but she thought maybe he was just nervous. She couldn't understand why he was paying the newspaper more attention than her. They both picked up their menus and began to read. She waited for a good minute in complete silence before deciding to try and start a conversation. 'So,' she said, 'have you eaten here before?'

'No,' replied Jonny, 'But I hear it's *shit, wank, bollocks.*'

'You chose it,' Janine said laughing.

He'd got away with it again. 'Well . . . you can't believe everything you hear,' he quipped. They laughed together. Jesus! He couldn't believe it. He was on a date and it was going well. A lot better than he could have ever imagined. He'd made a few mistakes, but so what? And so what if he was about to share a meal with an extra from close encounters of the fat kind. This felt good. This felt better than good.

The waiter approached, wondering why such a good looking bloke would be interested in such a gross-looking woman. He cleared his throat and prepared to speak in the French accent he'd been made to practice in the kitchen prior to walking out. It was his first day and he'd been warned that some of the customers could be a bit funny. He was prepared and focused. He didn't want to blow it. 'Good evening, monsieur et madam, will you be requiring any drinks zis evening?'

Janine wanted a glass of wine but couldn't pronounce any of the ones listed on the menu. She hoped Jonny would be paying, the menu seemed extortionate. 'Erm, could I just have a glass of dry house white, please?'

'Si.' *bastard!* The waiter hoped they hadn't noticed he'd just spoken Spanish and quickly said, 'And for monsieur?'

Jonny looked up from his menu and at the waiter; if he

was confident enough with his speech he'd definitely have made a comment about this being a French restaurant not a Paella bar. He decided it was safer to stick to the drink order. 'Can I have a bottle of *fuck*!'

A short but uncomfortable pause fell over the table. Janine wondered what the hell was going on and Jonny realised he'd just made a mistake he definitely couldn't talk himself out of. Fortunately, the waiter was on the ball and saved the day. 'Oh, Monsieur must mean the F.C.U.K. *Bon*. I'll bring zem right away.'

Janine laughed again, Jonny followed her lead. He was starting to get very hot under the collar though and felt it was only a matter of time before his luck ran out. He peered back down at his menu and decided it was for the best if he just sat quietly and tried to decode it.

God, this guy was hard work! Janine hated uncomfortable silences. She had already shared more than a few with him so far and they hadn't even got to the starters yet. She hoped they served big portions. She decided a good way to bring him out of his shell would be to ask a killer question. A big open question. Something that would provoke conversation and that he'd delight in answering. 'Well, Jonny,' she said, 'what do you like to do in your spare time? What are your most favourite things in the world?'

Jonny cleared his throat. Janine must be really interested in him. 'Well, mainly I like to *fuck, wank, spunk*!'

CHAPTER FOURTEEN

FRIDAY 22nd June – 9 p.m.

This was it. They were on. All three of them were psyched up and ready to rock. The butterflies in their stomachs had grown. They had a murder of angry crows in there trying to break free. They'd got on the same seventies gear they'd worn for the photo shoot. The shots had come out so fantastically that the band now considered the outfits lucky charms.

Martin grabbed his guitar and slung it over his shoulder, Steve put his sticks in the back pocket of his trousers and Jimbob grabbed his bass. They left the dressing room and found one of the backstage crew was waiting outside the door to escort them to the stage. Their room was the first changing room on the corridor, making it the furthest away from the stage entrance. The walk in front of them seemed like a mile.

As they set off, they could hear the crowd slowly getting louder and louder. The nerves grew. Martin looked back at the other two and was reassured to see they were as petrified as he was, but these were good nerves. Good, healthy nerves. Even so, Martin was unsure as to whether he'd manage to say hello to the crowd without stuttering or falling over. Taking Jimbob's sunglasses off him, he popped them on his own face. He could hardly see a thing. Perfect.

They continued the walk and reached the back door. The stage hand reached across to the handle, paused and said, 'OK, lads. Just go through here and there's some stairs, once you get to the top turn left and you're on the stage, as soon as you introduce yourselves that's the cue for the sound and lighting engineers. Good luck.'

As the door opened, the sound of the crowd hit them even harder. Martin realised they'd left the set list behind but was too nervous to care. They walked up the stairs and reached the top, then, terrified they walked onto the stage. It was so bright they couldn't even see the crowd. The venue wasn't illuminated at all and as they looked out at the audience, it just seemed as if a massive black curtain was in front of them. They could hear them though and as they made their way across the stage the cheers grew louder.

Martin walked over to the amplifier and plugged in his guitar. It immediately began feeding back and squealing, but before he could touch the dials two engineers turned up and sorted it out. It was the coolest thing he'd ever seen, he felt like a true rock star for the first time. He looked around at the other two, who had now taken their positions and were ready.

Martin walked towards the microphone at the front and, bursting with pressure said, 'Evening, Manchester. We're Jimbob Rifkin' The cheers grew louder still and he struck the A chord on his guitar. As he did so, the nerves instantly melted into every inch of his body and soul and turned into adrenaline. This was it, they'd made it, if they never did a gig this big again, it wouldn't matter. They'd tasted it, the adrenaline pumped around his veins producing the best high he'd ever known. Better than any drug, better than any girl, better than any fucking armed robbery.

As the chord rang out, Steve clicked his drumsticks and shouted, 'One! Two! Three! Four!' and they let rip. And they were fantastic.

Clive was beginning to regret doing the deal with Jerry earlier that day as they'd only been in the pub for two hours and he had not stopped going on about it. Clive had tried to talk them into going to watch Jimbob Rifkin in Manchester, to no avail and had to resort to making an excuse that he needed a few beers inside him before he could pluck up the courage to ask Doreen out, but, as he finished off his fourth pint, he realised that his excuse had just expired.

Fortunately, Jonny bought him a few extra minutes as he stormed into the pub to drown his sorrows after a terrible first date. Going to *The Nobody* was a safe bet, everybody in there knew him well enough not to hold it against him. Thank God. He approached the bar and said, 'Pint please, *fuck, twat.*'

Doreen promptly served him and as he paid her, Clive, eager to further delay the inevitable, shouted, 'Hi Jonny, fancy joining us?'

Tarquin was irritated. He hated that fucking weirdo. Why everybody else liked him so much was beyond him. Jonny mooched over to the table with a face longer than the Great Wall of China. 'Jesus Christ, Jonny!' said Jerry. 'What the fuck's wrong with you? You look like someone's shit in your pocket and you've just put your hand in it!'

Jonny took a seat between Clive and Tarquin, irritating Tarquin even further, and said, 'It's far, far worse than that.'

Tarquin leaned back and snapped, 'What?'

Jonny took a large swig from his pint then slammed it down on the table and said, 'I popped an ad in the *Gazette*. I've been on a *minge, fanny, twat*, date.'

Riz said what everybody else was thinking. 'So, what happened then?'

Jonny stared into his beer and replied, 'I fucked it up, *shit, knacker*. She asked me what I liked to do and my Tourette's kicked in and I told her I like to *funk, wank, spunk*. Fuck wank spunk.'

Jerry and Tarquin found this absolutely hilarious. Clive remained silent, but only because he was too busy trying to figure out what to say to Doreen once Jerry remembered their deal. Rizwan on the other hand tried to offer a little support. 'Surely she'd understand, Jonny. It's not like it's your fault.'

Jonny moved his glance away from his beer and across the table towards Rizwan, 'I wasn't going to tell her I have Tourette's.'

Tarquin and Jerry stopped laughing, half shocked half completely confused. Jerry asked the burning question, 'Why not?'

Jonny took another swig of his drink before saying, 'I didn't want her to know.'

The lads were trying not to laugh; how the fuck could she possibly not know? They all stared down at the table, knowing that if they caught a glimpse of each other they definitely wouldn't be able to contain it. Even Jerry had decided that to kick a man whilst he was so far down was wrong. Tarquin wasn't so sympathetic, though and said,

'So you'd rather she thought you liked to fuck, wank and spunk?'

This irritated Jonny; he was damned if he was going to be lectured to by a queen, 'Fuck off, Tarquin. I can deal with this *bastard, fucker*, involuntary speech disorder.'

Tarquin smiled and said, 'Yeah, it fucking sounds like it!'

Jonny wasn't taking this from him. 'Fuck off, you fucking arse bandit!'

This just amused Tarquin even more. 'You'll have to help me out here Jonny, was that on purpose or the Tourette's kicking in?'

Jonny stood up and threw the rest of his drink over Tarquin. 'Fuck off, you twat!'

Tarquin stood up shaking his head and his hands to remove the beer, but rather than being irritated, he found the fact that'd he'd managed to rattle Jonny to such an extent absolutely hilarious, and said, 'I'm still none the wiser!'

At this, Jonny stormed straight out of the pub. Tarquin took his seat again and realised that the rest of the group's frowning eyes were firmly fixed on him. Their stares burned right through him. 'What the fuck are you lot looking at?' he demanded irritably.

Surprisingly, it was Jerry who jumped to defend Jonny. 'That was a bit out of order, Tarquin.' The rest nodded in agreement, then all sat there quietly waiting for Tarquin to say something.

'What?' he asked. 'What the fuck do you want me to do?'

'You could go after him and say sorry,' said Clive.

'OK, I'll go after him. Fuck! You lot are a right bunch of pussies!' He reached into his pocket and threw some money on the table, 'This is the lottery money from the warehouse lot. Don't fucking spend it!'

Tarquin polished off his drink and stormed out of the pub. Jerry reached over to grab the money but Clive got to it first, saying, 'You, my friend, can't be trusted.' He picked it up and put it in his wallet. 'You'd better give me your share as well, I'll look after it.'

As Jerry pulled out his wallet and handed the money over, he suddenly remembered that Clive had some unfinished business to attend to. 'Haven't you forgotten something, Clivey boy?'

Never. He thought that business with Jonny might have distracted Jerry enough for him to let it drop. Realising he really had run out of excuses this time, he decided he'd just have to bite the big one and go for it. 'OK. OK. I'm going. I'll be back in a minute.'

The lads bounced off the stage in high spirits. They ran back to their dressing room to celebrate.

'That was absolutely, bar none, the most fucking unbelievable experience of my entire life!' Martin said, slumping down on one of the leather couches. Jimbob couldn't speak, he had tears in his eyes. Steve nodded in agreement and screamed, throwing his arms up into the air.

Jimbob went into the en-suite and came back with three bottles of Budweiser. He popped the tops using a bottle opener on his keyring and they raised their glasses to toast the performance.

They quickly downed the first bottle and as Martin got up to get another round, Jimbob removed a small bag of cocaine from his pocket and began chopping it up on the table. It was time to celebrate. Martin opened the beers and sat back down. He reached into his inside pocket and removed some weed, a packet of Benson and Hedges and some king-size Rizlas.

As they were making these party preparations, there came a knock at the door. They each quickly fired up a line and Martin put his ingredients back in his pocket. Steve walked towards the door and opened it slightly to reveal a beautiful looking blonde girl. She was about their age, close to six feet tall and dressed in a tight, low-cut top with an even tighter skirt.

'Can I help you?' asked Steve.

'Well . . . I just saw your set and really loved it. I came to congratulate you. Is it OK if I come in?'

'Hang on,' Steve said and closed the door.

'Who is it?' asked Jimbob.

'It's a fucking really fit bird wanting to congratulate us. Should I let her in?'

Martin couldn't believe his ears. 'Of course you should fucking let her in!'

Steve opened the door smiled and said, 'Yes. Come in.' As she walked into the room the lads' jaws dropped. She was unbelievable. Steve wandered outside and told the stage hand that they didn't want to be disturbed under any circumstances until the results were due to be announced.

As he came back into the room, Martin was getting the girl a beer. Jimbob had taken his coke back out and was at work making four large lines. They'd learned that her name was Jackie and she was from Birmingham. Although you wouldn't have been able to tell from her accent; she hardly had one at all.

Martin took his seat and once again began skinning up. 'So Jackie, what sort of celebration did you have in mind?' he asked.

Jackie said nothing, she just simply removed the tight top she had been wearing to reveal a pair of large, perfect breasts.

Clive stood up and walked calmly towards the bar. The other two sat back to watch. Jerry had been looking forward to this all day. Clive placed his open wallet down on the bar and ordered the drinks from Doreen. This was it. No going back.

In the far corner of the pub Paul had just had a sip of milk. Theodore turned to look at him and asked, 'Have you seen how much money there is in that wallet over there?'

Paul glanced towards Clive's open wallet on the bar and replied, 'Yeah.'

Theodore spoke to him again. 'Why don't you go get that money while I look after these drinks?'

That bear was always getting him into trouble. Paul looked down at Theodore shaking his head. 'No. I can't. It's wrong.'

Theodore was quick to encourage him, 'No it's not. We need that money.'

Paul was adamant, 'No. It's stealing,' he said. He could tell Theodore was getting angry and impatient.

'Come on, Paul! It isn't stealing if you need it more than they do. Hurry up. Or we'll miss our chance!'

Paul didn't want to do this but he knew what'd happen if he didn't. Theodore would keep nagging and nagging until it drove him insane. He had no other option. He sighed, picked up Theodore and headed off towards the bar. The regulars were so used to him wandering around aimlessly that they just completely ignored him. Riz and Jerry had got so bored with watching Clive and waiting for him to make his move that they were now deep in conversation and didn't realise what Paul was up to, either. Jerry noticed him walk past their table as he left, though and felt a lot more relaxed once he'd gone.

Clive was on fire. He was surprised how well he'd dealt with it. Not only had he got the date but Doreen had bought the round. He was so pleased he didn't even notice his wallet had been emptied as he picked it up and put it into his pocket. He strutted back to the table with the drinks, placed each of them down, took a seat and casually took a sip from his glass.

'Well?' asked Jerry, looking forward to hearing how badly it all went.

'We're going out next Friday.' Proclaimed Clive, raising his glass to toast his success.

What the fuck? How the hell did he manage that? It was bad enough that Clive had got the date, but Jerry was fucked if he was going to sit in here all night and listen to him going on about it, so he said 'That loony's just left.'

Rizwan leaned forward. 'I heard another rumour about him.'

Fantastic! Now Clive wouldn't be able to gloat for a few minutes. 'Do tell,' said Jerry.

'I heard that he fell in love with a bloke called Theodore, they'd arranged to have a surrogate child through some lesbian friend of theirs and after this Theodore feller got her up the duff, realised they were straight and fucked off together. That's why he went mad.'

This was the strangest one yet. Jerry had a few views to share with them, and with Tarquin out of the way this seemed like the ideal time. 'Now, I'm not homophobic . . . or gay, but I don't think its right for gay couples to be having children.'

'Why not?' asked Clive.

'Because . . . children are cruel . . . and they're bright. They bully each other at school, and they notice things . . . they tend to notice if your mum's called Derek.'

Steve was lying naked on the floor with Jackie riding him furiously. The other two were pissed off that he'd got stuck in first. Jimbob wasn't letting it bother him too much; he undid his trousers, whipped out his chopper and began stroking it whilst he watched.

Martin was a little bit shocked by this for two reasons; firstly, Jimbob's cock was massive and secondly, it felt extremely uncomfortable sitting next to a mate who was wanking; it was just a bit too gay. 'What the fuck are you doing?' he asked.

Jimbob paused for a moment, looked at Martin and then glanced down at his cock. 'What does it fucking look like I'm doing? I'm knocking one out!'

Martin pointed over at Jackie and Steve going hell for leather on the floor and said, 'You'll get your turn.'

Jimbob was pissed off. He was relieving himself so he could last a bit longer when his turn came around. The cocaine pulsing through his body was making him randy as hell and he just wanted to fuck her all over like Steve was doing. 'Bollocks to this,' he said and stood up. He started to remove his clothes. This irritated Martin even more as he was right in his view of Jackie. Jimbob had had the right idea, though. Once naked, he went over and put his cock in her mouth. She didn't seem to mind. In fact she seemed to be enjoying it.

Bastard! thought Martin, wishing he'd done that. He thought they were taking it in turns. He was too annoyed to get aroused as he saw her riding Steve and sucking Jimbob, who had now got her to lean down on top of Steve so he didn't have to stand up anymore. The lazy bastard.

Fuck it, thought Martin and racked himself up another fat line, fired it up his nose top speed and got up to have a look around the action. Once around the back, watching Steve's cock banging in and out of her, he got an idea. He'd just have to stick it up her arse.

He removed his clothes, never once taking his eye off the prize and tried to think of the best way to do this. He decided it was probably best to adopt a sumo wrestler type pose with his legs, stand above her and work it out from there.

He knew if he went straight for it he'd probably hurt her and ruin it for everybody, so he decided on a little bit of gentle persuasion. As he licked his fingers and began slowly rubbing her arse, he couldn't help but think he'd got the bum deal. She seemed to like it though; she was making a bit more noise. Well, as much noise as she could make with Jimbob's massive cock in her mouth. He gently slid a finger inside her. It felt weird, he could feel Steve's piece pumping in and out, just a small piece of flesh separating his finger from Steve's knob. What worried him more was the fact that Steve actually seemed to like it. He put it out of his mind, slowly slid in another finger and after a minute or so of warming her up he decided she was ready.

Slowly and carefully, he kept trying to put himself inside her, but every time he managed to get it in, Steve's inward thrust would push him back out again. After the tenth attempt it had started to get annoying, so he lowered his stance a bit more and just went for it. That was it, that was better, he and Steve had managed to get a bit of a rhythm going, too. It was actually working. Steve moves out, he moves in, perfect. Who'd have thought their talent for timing could have paid off in such a way?

Steve had put up with it for as long as he could stand. He'd tried to ignore it but it was distracting him a little bit too much. 'Martin!' he whispered loudly. He didn't notice, he was banging away merrily with a massive smile on his face, 'Martin!' Steve said again.

Martin leaned to his right, where he could see Steve's face popping out from underneath Jackie. Her massive tits were slapping him around the side of the head as she backed onto their cocks. 'What?' asked Martin.

Steve couldn't believe he even needed to ask. 'Your fucking balls are touching mine!'

Tarquin was sat at home alone. He'd not gone back to the pub that evening after they'd made him go and say sorry to Jonny. He hadn't said sorry, either. He saw him in the car park and considered belting ten balls of shit out of him, but didn't apologise. He also didn't fancy going back into the pub because he couldn't risk them wanting to go to the club again. If he'd been seen by any-body who really knew him, other than Jimbob, everything would have been ruined in an instant. He was getting extremely bored with having to hang around with such a bunch of losers. Something was going to have to give. And quickly.

Jimbob Rifkin were in a really bad state. Stoned, coked and pissed out of their tiny minds. They had just been called to go to the stage as it was time to announce the winner. They'd definitely made it into the top three because only the top three had to go up there and wait to hear the results.

They swiftly got rid of Jackie and tried to compose themselves a little before heading out. The walk would give them a good few minutes to get their shit together. As they got nearer the stage and heard the crowd, Martin realised that staying clean for the performance had definitely been a good idea. He was feeling too coked up and arrogant to give a fuck about a crowd full of people now and going up there seemed like a chore rather than an adventure.

Steve and Jimbob felt similarly; at exactly that point, each of them had made an unspoken bond never to take drugs prior to a performance, a bond that they would stick to religiously even though none of them would ever mention it.

They also made an unspoken bond that if they ever had the opportunity of a threesome again, it would probably work out best to take it in turns. Jimbob would have to go last though, due to the size of his knob.

They went through the bottom door and made their way up the stairs. As they reached the stage, Planet Lounge were already up there, and a band they didn't recognise. They got a loud cheer from the audience and strutted across to the far left of the stage. The compère for the evening was the singer from last year's winning band. He grabbed a mike from one of the stands at the front and said, 'OK, ladies and gentlemen, I think you'll all agree we've seen eight fantastic bands this evening.'

The pissed-up crowd cheered and heckled. 'Our judges have chosen a winner and consider the three acts we have up here are the best of the bunch tonight. There can only be one winner though, so let's see who it is.'

As he pulled the silver envelope from his inside pocket, Jimbob Rifkin stood there cool as three cucumbers. They were pretty confident. They knew they'd played their best, they couldn't have done any better than they did.

'And the winner is ... Planet Lounge, ladies and gentlemen.'

Planet-fucking-Lounge? The lads were shocked but not overly disappointed. They'd had the best gig of their entire life and they weren't going to let not winning ruin it. They knew they'd played a blinder and they'd got down to the last three. They realised that winning this wasn't the be-all and end-all; the guy stood up there compèring was still a nobody and his band were still nowhere. They also knew that Planet Lounge were a bunch of cunts, so, as they left them on stage to perform an encore, Martin came up with an idea.

On the way back down the stairs, he told the rest of the band his plan and they walked down the corridor giggling like naughty school boys. Once the stage hand had dropped them off at their dressing room, they waited for a moment before opening their door to make sure nobody was around. Then they quietly walked back down the corridor and into Planet Lounge's dressing room.

They were disappointed to see that it was quite a bit bigger than theirs and this simply reinforced in their minds that what they were about to do wasn't wrong or cruel, it was one hundred percent justified. Martin went into their fridge and removed as many bottles of beer as he could carry. Jimbob popped the tops and they began drinking about a third out of each bottle before pissing in them, securing the tops back on and putting them back into the fridge.

Before they left, Steve had one more trick up his sleeve. Their drummer didn't drink, and he was one of these vegetarian herbal tea-drinking types, so it was only fair that he didn't miss out on the treat they'd left behind for his band mates. Steve grabbed the kettle, emptied the water into the sink and pissed in that as well. He'd briefly considered spiking it with an E but that would have just been a waste of good drugs – plus, with the amount of toxins buzzing around their bodies, they'd probably end up spannered by drinking the piss, anyway.

As they got back into the room and flopped down onto the sofa, they felt pleased with how the night had turned out as a whole. The pills had left Martin's mouth feeling uncomfortably dry and he removed a small breath freshener spray from his pocket and fired a couple of blasts into his mouth. That did the trick nicely. 'Here, can I have a go with that?' asked Jimbob.

Martin nodded and passed it across. However, rather than opening his mouth and spraying it in, Jimbob fired a shot up his left nostril, then fell off the sofa onto the floor and started convulsing. The other two panicked. *The fucking idiot!* thought Martin. What the hell had he done that for?

'Are you all right?' asked Steve. 'Jimbob!'

Jimbob sat upright and opened his eyes. His pupils were fully dilated and as black as Darth Vader's cape. He panted for a moment, 'That were fucking brilliant!'

CHAPTER FIFTEEN

FRIDAY 29th June – 8 a.m.

Jerry had been looking forward to the thirtieth of May for weeks. He'd made his excuses in advance and booked today as a holiday from work. This was a treat and delight he enjoyed too much to let the novelty to wear off.

He'd been shopping, purchasing a few special items here and there in preparation for today and as he lay there, watching GMTV, he felt almost overwhelmingly content. It seemed a shame to get up and out of bed, but he knew he had to. He had far more important things to do.

He dragged himself out of bed, put on his dressing gown and pottered downstairs into the kitchen, where he opened his junk drawer under the kettle and removed five tea light candles before fumbling around for a lighter. Once he'd got it, he loaded everything into his pockets and headed back upstairs into the bathroom. He carefully placed the tea lights around the bath; firstly, each of the front corners, one by the mirror and one by the soap dish.

Then the back corners, one by his shaving foam, and one by his razor. Then he finished off his arrangement by placing one at the front in the middle, between the taps.

He paused for a moment and thought about the Friday before. He'd not seen anything of Jonny T since Tarquin had had a go at him. He thought that before he got involved with his self indulgence, he should give him a call, just to make sure he was all right, so he walked back into his bedroom, picked up the phone and called him.

'Hi, Jonny, it's me, Jerry. Listen, I was just ringing up to make sure you're all right. I've not seen you in the pub since that gay bastard had a go at you.'

'Oh, I'm fine, mate. I've just been *fuck, cunt, twat* busy.'

'Cool. Here, listen. Why don't you get on the internet on some of them dating sites? They're fucking great. I joined up to one, thirteen quid for a quarter and got loads of fanny.'

'Yeah? How does it work?'

'Basically, girls enter for free, they put a picture on and a profile and you look for which one you want.'

'And you got a guaranteed *fuck, shag, twat*, fuck?'

'Well, not at first, I was aiming a bit too high. I started off by going for the young, good-looking ones but I didn't get any joy. Just ended up taking them on the piss all night, or to posh restaurants with no shag at the end. So I decided to change tactics and moved on to the older ones. The divorcees. I'd turn up, give them a bit of a sob story about just coming out of a long term relationship, put the cards on the table, tell them I wasn't interested in anything serious so soon, just looking for a bit of fun, and bang! Straight back to theirs for a shag.'

'Sounds all right, but if it's so good, how come you're not doing it now?'

'I got a bit addicted to it, had to wean myself of it.'

'Didn't you ever turn up and there was some pig-ugly bird there?'

'You have to take the rough with the smooth, mate. There was this one time I turned up and the woman was about sixty, she must have put a thirty-year-old picture on the website. Cheeky bitch.'

'So what did you do?'

'Well, I thought bollocks to it. I'd travelled sixty miles so I fucked her, anyway.'

'Urgh,' laughed Jonny, 'What was it like?'

'Surprisingly good, actually.'

'I don't know *fuck, twat, shit*, anything about computers though.'

'Try video dating then, there's one just outside town. Or go to a Paul McKenna weight loss seminar.'

'A what?'

'Paul McKenna weight loss seminar. Full of fanny, wall to wall.'

'But I'm not fat.'

'Nor are half of them. They just think they're fat. And anyway, there's nowt wrong with the fat ones. Get yourself booked on one of them and go pull yourself a chunkie. It's perfect, they might be a bit fat so they'll have to forgive you for the Tourette's, but you've got yourself an investment there for the future.'

'How?'

'Well, stick with her and there's about an eighty percent chance she'll lose the weight.'

Jonny laughed. 'Ta, Jerry. I needed *fuck, cunt, fadge*, cheering up. Think I'll just stick to the video thing. I've got another one from the Gazette lined up for next week, anyway.'

'Nice one, where you off to? Anywhere nice?'

'Nah, think I'll take your advice. I went for nice last time and it got me nowhere. I'm going to think of somewhere loud, where I don't have to talk.'

'Well, good luck mate. Let me know how you get on.'

'Will do. See you.'

Jerry put the phone down and headed back to the bathroom. He put the plug in and started the bath running, just hot water at first, to make the room nice and steamy. Whilst it powered into the empty bath, he added small amount of lavender oil. Beautiful. He removed his robe and sat down on the toilet to soak up the scent and the warmth of the bathroom whilst applying his face pack.

Clive was nervous as hell as he left for work that morning. Tonight might finally be the night he kissed his virginity goodbye. For real. He had been hard at work masturbating all week to build up his stamina and figured he'd probably have the opportunity to squeeze in a few more tries at work. He couldn't imagine anything worse than not being able to last the distance.

Once the bath had reached a third full, Jerry started the cold tap running, adding a little more lavender. He patiently waited and monitored the flow until it reached the desired temperature. Once this was achieved, he picked the lighter out of his discarded robe and lit the candles.

He slowly lowered himself into the warm water and leaned back, feeling relaxed and marvellous. He glanced down at his hairy legs and wondered how much nicer it'd feel later on if they weren't so hairy. If they weren't hairy at all. He hesitated for a moment; was he seriously considering shaving his fucking legs? Why not? He never wore shorts, nobody would ever see them. He lifted out his leg and moved it over to the bottom corner of the bath, almost burning his foot on the candle.

Once he'd got comfortable, he took his shaving foam and added a thin layer to his leg, then took his razor and began to slowly and carefully shave his leg, every inch from top to bottom. He repeated this process with the other and grew a little confused about where to stop. He looked down at the bright ginger bush of pubic hair he had surrounding his cock and realised how stupid it looked now that he had shaved his legs. Before, they kind of blended in, but now he looked like he had some sort of mad luminous afro strapped on his member. He decided it was probably for the best to just whip his pubes off as well. He left himself a small thin strip in the middle so that the hair coming down from his bellybutton didn't just stop dead randomly and decided it was probably best to get out of the bath now. The water had gone pretty cold by this time and it looked like ginger hair soup.

He dried himself off, put his robe back on and went into his bedroom. Once there, he opened up his wardrobe. He didn't have many clothes; a couple of suits, a few shirts and a few pairs of jeans, but as he pushed the hangers aside he revealed a small shelf housing a decorative pink shoe box. He lifted it out and placed it carefully on the bed, then slowly removed the lid to reveal the purchases he'd made in preparation.

For starters, he removed a bottle of toner, a couple of cotton wool balls and some moisturiser. He turned around to face the mirror on his back wall and realised he'd forgotten to remove his face pack. Idiot. He went back through to the bathroom and washed it off before returning to his spot in front of the mirror. Then he carefully poured a small amount of toner onto one of the cotton wool balls and meticulously wiped every inch of his face before discarding it and moisturising.

Next came the main course. He picked out the lipstick, turned around to face the mirror again and applied it carefully. He was impressed; berry tint was definitely his colour.

Then dessert. He wished he'd not bought so many, it was hard to decide which pair to choose. He decided to read each packet; one of them would definitely appeal once he'd done his research. After a few minutes of browsing, he decided on the Pretty Polly ones as the packaging claimed: *These stylish 15 denier tights boast a reinforced body, an open gusset, smooth sheer legs and a reinforced toe.* They were also black; his favourite.

Jerry carefully removed them from the packaging, size fourteen. He hoped he'd fit into them. He'd been following Paul McKenna's regime for weeks in order to get out of a sixteen and couldn't believe the lads were still calling him a fat bastard.

He tidied away the toner, lipstick, moisturiser and the box, then lay down on the bed. He gathered up the left leg of the tights, carefully placed his toes inside and then slowly pulled them up towards the knee. He was amazed by how smooth and soft they felt; it was like pulling pure silk over his legs.

Jerry arched his back, lifting his backside up from the bed and slowly pulled the tights up to his waist. Amazing. He was in heaven; he'd never felt pleasure like it. He sat up and peered down, and gleefully but carefully inspected his legs. He started at his toes and slowly worked upwards. As he got to his shins, he twisted his leg to examine his calves, then his thighs, then continued onward to his almost bald erection which was now proudly protruding from the open gusset.

The novelty of last week's gig had quickly worn off and Jimbob was crashing down to earth with a bang. Today was his final chance to get the money and he had nothing to give. Last week's celebrations had simply added another three hundred pounds on to his debt, not that he was going to let Maz find out. He knew he'd have to go and ask the lads for the cash and decided he'd try to tap them up for some extra whilst he was there; he needed to show up with at least something. Another goodwill gesture might just save him from getting beaten to a bloody pulp.

He decided that now that the battle of the bands was out of the way, he'd have to sell his bass guitar and amp. He could always buy them back later or get new ones on hire purchase. The band were enjoying a few weeks of well-earned rest and recuperation, so the others might not even need to find out.

Even if the best case scenario had happened and he managed to get the three hundred from Steve and Martin, plus borrowing another hundred from each of them and then managed to sell his equipment for five hundred, that would still leave him owing Maz the best part of a grand. He had about twelve hours or so to find it, and time was ticking away.

CHAPTER SIXTEEN

FRIDAY 29th June – 1 p.m.

Tarquin left S-Packers to head down to the café. He'd hated lunchtimes lately; at least Rizwan provided a little company. Their hours had moved slightly and the new lot he was working with were even more annoying and a damn sight more boring.

As he reached the end of the car park and approached the main road, he hoped to hell he wouldn't get sprung in the café; that was the last thing he needed. He knew the rest of the lads were working but you never knew who could be watching or listening.

He went in and ordered a bacon sandwich. She was there waiting in the corner as she promised she would be. He grabbed his buttie took a seat and said to Doreen, in a voice that wasn't camp or northern anymore, 'Right. What's so fucking important that you'd risk blowing everything by meeting me here?'

'I'm not so sure about all this anymore,' she replied.

He couldn't fucking believe it; after all this effort and hard work he'd had to put in, he was fucked if she was caving in now. 'It's all right for you, Doreen! You told me he was gay! If I can put up with acting camp for six months to get a result, you can surely manage a few dates.'

A few? A few! She wasn't intending on dragging this out any longer. If she was going to do it at all, it would have to be sooner rather than later. 'Bollocks, Tarquin. If you really want me to do it, it'll have to be tonight.'

Stupid bitch. All the hard work and preparation that had gone into this and she was getting impatient now. When they'd come so close! 'You'll scare him off! You know what's at stake, Doreen. A cellar full of readies, that's what that guy said. That crazy old bitch is sitting on a fortune. We can't risk scaring him off now. We're nearly there.'

Doreen already had it figured out though. 'Look, you said he was a virgin, right?' Tarquin nodded. 'So I'll convince him not to take me out for a meal, get back to his, shag him senseless, really knacker him out then, when he's shot his muck, rolled over and fallen asleep, I'll get it. It's now or never, Tarquin. Non-negotiable.'

He hoped this scenario would work out as he wanted, because he'd put far too much effort in for it all to go wrong now. He was also acutely aware that he was on borrowed time as far as his fake identity was concerned. If

Jimbob had ever seen him acting overly camp when he dropped off the drugs, everything would have been ruined for sure. Perhaps Doreen had it right. They should just get it over and done with and get out of Holme Bridge as quickly as possible.

Jonny had been trying the woman at the dating agency's patience for long enough and she was relieved that his lunch hour was over and he'd had to return to his car lot. Taking the video had initially started out fantastic. The camera loved him. He had naturally olive skin, piercing blue eyes and gorgeous long dark hair. She'd quite fancied him herself, until he opened his mouth. Why he wanted her to cover up his affliction in the editing suite was completely beyond her; surely it made more sense to just be honest about these things?

As she sat reviewing his tape, she couldn't help but feel sorry for him; it was always such a shame when ordinary, nice people were marred with an affliction. She also saw so many really pleasant people come through the doors who enjoyed little success and got left on the shelf purely because they weren't good looking enough.

On the flip-side of the coin, she also had a lot of good-looking people coming in that were absolute bastards.

Surely it was they who should have the afflictions or the not-so-perfect features. At least they deserved it.

She was a professional, though and prided herself on her matchmaking skills. It might take her a while but she'd find the right person for him. Somebody who was as beautifully flawed as he was. Somebody who wouldn't care about his affliction and would like him simply for being himself. She'd have her work cut out, though. But, as she reviewed his tape and admired his looks, she came up with an idea . . .

As the boys ploughed another pound into the fruit machine, they couldn't understand why they never won. Their mum had given them four twenty-pound bags of pound coins and they were nearly finished. Although the light the machine generated was more than welcome, as was the novelty of being able to do something new, the fruit machine had actually ruined their enjoyment of hide and seek. One small, cold room and a few barrels offered little in the way of hiding space. It wouldn't be so bad if the machine actually plugged in down there, but the cable ran all the way upstairs and out of the door. It did get turned off and on occasionally, probably by 'him'.

As they heard footsteps approaching the door, they

paused; those weren't their mother's footsteps, they were too heavy. Perhaps they'd finally get to see *him*. They were nervous as they heard the door unlock and as it opened, they glanced up the stairs. Thanks to the fruit machine, they no longer had to hide their eyes when the door opened and they saw him. For the first time in their lives. Billy thought he looked exactly like Bobby, Bobby thought he looked exactly like Billy would look if he had two arms and two legs; same pointy chin and small nose. There was one major difference, other than the obvious; he sported a huge beer belly which hung below the belt line of his trousers. It wobbled as he made his way down the stairs.

The boys didn't move or say anything, they were in shock. They moved away from the machine and each sat on a barrel. Dave didn't even give them a glance as he approached the fruit machine. He just simply knelt down, removed a key from his pocket and opened up a panel at the base of it.

He then removed a large blue cash bag from his back pocket and began lifting handfuls of pound coins from the bottom of the machine. He emptied it, replaced the panel, locked it again and then walked back up the stairs, out of the cellar and locked the door behind him.

Bobby glanced across at Billy and broke the silence. 'Charming. The first time we see him. The first time in our entire lives and he just wobbles in, takes the money, and fucks off!'

'What if it wasn't him?' asked Billy.

'Of course it was him. It had to be, they aren't going to want anybody to know we're locked down here.'

Billy couldn't understand Bobby's negativity and tried to reassure him. 'Come on Bobby, it's nobody's fault, we're just bad for business, that's all.'

'That's rubbish. We're prisoners, that's what we are. You can tell when Mum comes down that she's not happy about all this. It's wrong!'

Billy quickly tried to change the subject to something a bit more optimistic and pleasant. 'What do you think it's like out there?' he asked.

'I don't know,' replied his brother, 'but we'll find out, Billy. I'll find a way to get us out of here. I promise.'

Jimbob felt uncomfortable asking the lads for the cash but he had to do what he had to do. As he approached Martin's house, he felt ashamed at the state he'd managed to get himself into. Selling his amp and guitar to pay for drugs; it made him no better than a fucking smack head. He'd managed to get four hundred pounds in total for them, a little worse than he'd expected.

He stopped the car and got out, trying to think of an excuse for needing to borrow the extra cash. Nothing was coming. He'd simply have to make something up. He approached the front door and knocked loudly.

Inside, the knocking woke Martin up; he'd fallen asleep in front of the television. He dragged himself up and answered the door. 'Hiya, Jimmy boy. How you doing? Come in.' Jimbob followed Martin back through to the living room and sat next to him on the sofa.

Jimbob thought it best to get the unpleasant part out of the way and said, 'I need to get some cash off you, mate, for the coke we had last week after the gig.'

'No problem,' replied Martin, 'how much do you need?'

'Well, we burned through a fucking quarter of the stuff, one hundred and fifty's your share.'

'Fuck! How did we managed to get through that much? Jesus Christ! No wonder you need it. I've got some cash upstairs; I'll get it for you now.'

That was a lot less painful than Jimbob expected, he decided at that point he should just level with Martin, 'fess up, put all his cards on the table. 'Martin,' he said, 'I'm in really big trouble and I need your help. I don't know what to do.' Jimbob couldn't control his emotions anymore and tears started streaming down his face.

Martin felt a little uncomfortable, but Jimbob was his bass player, they had a bond that most people would never understand. When you're in a band with somebody, it makes you closer than family, each of you share a responsibility and a trust to make the whole thing work like a well-oiled machine. 'What do you need me to do?' he asked.

'I need money,' sobbed Jimbob, 'I'd been taking loads of coke I was supposed to be selling and I owe fifteen hundred quid to Maz, eighteen hundred including what we shoved up our noses last weekend. If I don't have the full amount by the end of today, he's told me he'll break my fucking fingers and toes. I've sold my bass and amp for four hundred quid but that still leaves me with over a grand to find! I don't know what to do.'

'Look,' said Martin, 'we'll sort something out. What about the money from the robbery?'

'I paid him that the same day, it bought me two weeks' grace.'

'Well, I kept my share. I felt funny about spending it, it's all I've got really, I'm skint but you can have it. It's probably best that you don't tell Steve about this though. He'll hit the fucking roof if he finds out.'

'I know, but I still need him to pay for the coke he took last week.'

'I'll speak to Steve and get you the one-fifty off him. I'll meet you in *The Nobody* tonight at seven and if I can come up with anything else I'll let you know. Don't worry, if I can't, with what you've got from your bass, my five hundred and Steve's cash, you'll definitely be turning up there with over half the debt. I'm sure it'll buy you another couple of weeks.'

'Thanks, Martin. I'll pay you back, I promise.'

'I don't want it back. Just get this fucking debt settled, get your bass back and quit dealing. A job should make you money, not lose you money.'

If only it was that simple. This wasn't like a normal job where you could simply hand in your notice and leave. He was tied. He knew too much.

CHAPTER SEVENTEEN

FRIDAY 29th June – 7 p.m.

Clive waited at the bus station in a state of nervous anticipation. His first ever date was almost upon him and he hoped he'd have enough to say. He and Doreen had shared more than a few uncomfortable silences across the bar at the pub and he hoped that trend would be bucked this evening. He'd decided that taking her for a meal or going to the cinema was probably the safest way keeping out of that problem, as you can't talk while there's a film on or your mouth is full of food.

Poor Clive had no idea what would be in store for him later that evening, but by the same token, as Doreen turned the corner and approached him, she too would never be able to guess quite how the evening would turn out.

'Hi Clive,' she said. 'How are you?'

'I'm fine, what do you fancy doing? I thought we could maybe go to the pictures or for a meal,' he replied.

Doreen couldn't be arsed with pissing around in a

cinema or eating for hours, she wanted to get on with it. She also wasn't overly keen on the idea of being seen out with Clive. He looked like a real geek. He'd obviously made an effort because he reeked of Brut aftershave and had clean fingernails, but his dress sense still left a lot to be desired; chinos hadn't been in fashion for years. 'I thought we might just go back to your place,' she said.

Dave loved sitting in front of his monitors, carefully surveying every inch of his empire. As he looked around the pub he saw Paul sat with Theodore. Theodore looked different though, he had a big golden medallion, some new clothes and an expensive-looking watch. Paul seemed to get weirder every week.

He panned around to Jimbob who was sat on his own without a drink; Dave thought he'd give him another few minutes before he called Shirley to throw him out. He also noticed that Jerry, Rizwan and Tarquin were a man short. Everything was perfect; all clean, tidy and organised. The place actually seemed to run more smoothly without Doreen there.

Martin entered the pub, ordered two pints of lager and took a seat next to Jimbob, who was silently praying he'd managed to come up with something. Martin placed a pint in front of him and said, 'I'm sorry, mate. I've managed to scrape together about another twenty quid but that's the lot, unfortunately. Have you managed to find anything?'

'No,' replied Jimbob, 'I just hope this is enough. Cheers, Martin. I won't ever forget this.'

'Don't worry about it; I wouldn't be much of a fucking mate if I let you get your fingers and toes chopped off.'

CHAPTER EIGHTEEN

FRIDAY 29th June – 9 p.m.

As they got to Clive's doorstep, he told Doreen that she needed to be quiet when they went in so as not to disturb his mother. He carefully unlocked the door and opened it. Instantly, the smell made Doreen feel ill. It was disgusting; she couldn't understand why Clive didn't notice it.

As they entered the house, Clive carefully closed the door behind him, removed Doreen's jacket and hung it up. As he turned to face her, she kissed him passionately, his first kiss. It felt different to how he'd expected, but in a good way. He hoped he was doing it right.

Doreen couldn't believe how badly he kissed; it was like having a knackered washing machine suck on your face. This, combined with the smell, wasn't doing anything for the queasy feeling in her stomach. She needed to get this bit over with as quickly as possible and decided to take the initiative. She pulled away from him and asked, 'Which is your room?'

Clive stood there with a smile on his face and an erection trying to bust out of his chinos. He pointed up the stairs and said, 'The first door at the top.'

She grabbed his hand and slowly guided him up the stairs. As she opened the door to his bedroom she couldn't believe her eyes. His room was plastered with various horror movie posters and newspaper clippings. He had a single bed complete with *Star Wars* duvet cover. It looked like your typical thirteen-year-old's bedroom. At least it didn't smell quite as bad in there though.

Clive closed the door and suggested a little music. Then he dimmed the lights and moved towards her. She couldn't face another kiss from him so she jumped straight onto the bed and said, 'Come on then, Clive. Come over here and fuck me.'

Jimbob stood outside Maz's office. He'd been there for a good twenty minutes and hadn't managed to pluck up the courage to go inside. He didn't know why he was delaying the inevitable, he knew he should just go in, pay the money and keep his fingers crossed. If they were still in one piece . . .

He was seven hundred and thirty pounds short. Pulling back so much of the debt was a massive achievement and he just hoped it would be enough. He composed himself and knocked on the door. There was no point in delaying it anymore, the earlier he did this, the less chance there would be of Maz being pissed or coked up.

'Who is it?' came Maz's mock Jamaican voice from behind the door.

'It's me. Jimbob.'

He opened the door and walked towards Maz's desk. Two of the bouncers were in there with him. Jimbob thought Maz might send them away but he didn't, just simply offered Jimbob a rolled-up note and asked him to help himself to a line.

That was the last thing Jimbob wanted but he knew a refusal would look bad and he didn't want to piss him off any further. 'Thanks,' he said and snorted a small line. He'd not taken any for over a week and it hit him instantly. He didn't get a buzz from it though, just an overwhelming wave of paranoia.

'Well, Jimmy man. Do you have good news for me or bad news for you?' Maz stood up, he didn't like being seated when he spoke to somebody. He liked to be looking down on them.

'A bit of both, Maz,' trembled Jimbob.

'You'd better tell me how good the good news is then. Might put me in a better mood.' Maz looked at the bouncer to his left and laughed.

'I've got a thousand and seventy quid. I'm still short.' Jimbob couldn't even look at Maz as he placed the money on his desk; he just hung his head and stared down at his shoes.

'Well,' said Maz. 'This gives us a little bit of a problem, doesn't it, Jimmy man?'

'I can get the rest, I just nee – ' He couldn't even finish his sentence before Maz shouted, 'I'm fucking sick of your excuses and I'm fucking sick of giving you time! People around here are starting to think I've gone fucking soft, man! Giving you all this extra time to find me the money. Your time has run out, Jimmy. You owe me seven fucking fingers or seven fucking toes!'

Jimbob's heart sank. This was it, game over. Definitely no more chances. He knew there was absolutely no point in trying to negotiate anymore, he was left with only two options, not being able to play bass again, or not being able to walk again. He looked at his hands trying to find a suitable way out; as long as he kept his thumb, index finger and little finger on his left hand, he'd still be able to hold the notes on his bass. On his right, he could make do with even less, just a thumb and finger were all he needed to hold a plectrum, but that only added up to five so he would have to lose two toes as well. Did he go for both little toes, with them being the least useful, or try and keep the damage to one foot? Whatever it was he needed to make his mind up quickly as Maz had just handed a hammer to one of the bouncers.

As Clive was shagging Doreen, his mind wasn't properly on the job in hand. Rather than concentrating on his technique, he was too busy looking down at Doreen's naked body, trying to remember every inch of it so that if he never got to have sex again at least he'd have everything securely stored in his memory for the next few hundred wanks.

He was also finding it difficult to concentrate because of the noise she was making. He couldn't understand why she needed to be so loud. She was drowning out Take That's *A Million Love Songs* and it was his favourite. He grabbed the pillow from under her head and gently placed it across her face to muffle the sounds. That was better, he could concentrate properly now. With everything safely and neatly stored in his brain and the moaning neatly muffled, he began to really go for it. It was much better than he'd expected.

The larger of the two bouncers carried a passed-out Jimbob down the fire exit at the back of the club and placed him on the back seat of his car. They had neatly tied his hands and feet up with plastic bags to contain the bleeding. As Jimbob drifted in and out of consciousness, he wondered if he'd survive. He couldn't feel any pain, his hands and his feet were completely numb.

As the bouncer got into the driving seat and accelerated quickly away, he kept glancing back at Jimbob to make sure there wasn't any blood escaping and leaking onto his seats as he powered towards the hospital. He couldn't believe Maz could be so despicable.

Jimbob's face was getting whiter by the second, his colour slowly fading away as the blood from his busted fingers and toes slowly pumped into the bags. Drifting back into consciousness, he tried to figure out where he was, he couldn't move. He felt paralysed; his face was hanging over the edge of the back seat staring straight into the foot well.

He wondered how he would ever explain this away and what his parents would think of him if they ever found out. Maz had done a real number on Jimbob; if the band didn't succeed in making it, the only thing he would be good for was drug-dealing. He certainly wouldn't be able to manage a job that involved manual labour and any job that involved using a computer was definitely out of the question. He was also unsure of what to tell the hospital, not that it would matter as he drifted away into unconsciousness once more.

The bouncer pulled up at the Accident and Emergency entrance of the hospital, got out of the car, opened the back door and pulled Jimbob out of the car and onto the floor. Then he quickly got back into his car and drove away at speed, hoping he'd make it through all right.

As Clive came, he felt amazing. He was proud he'd lasted so long and must have done a good job because towards the end Doreen had been wriggling around all over and screaming at the top of her voice. He was glad he'd kept the pillow there to muffle the noise, but as he removed it, Doreen's blue, lifeless face stared up at him.

Shocked, he immediately withdrew from her and slapped her around the face. 'Doreen! Doreen!' He was getting no response. He laid his head on her chest to listen for a heartbeat. Nothing. He couldn't believe what he'd done.

He got up, pulled his chinos back on, flicked off the music and then paced the bedroom trying to think of what to do. This one was definitely going to leave a trail. He wouldn't mind, but this one had been an accident.

He'd pretty much run out of places to hide the bodies and knew he'd have to start thinking of a few ways to dispose of them. The first one to go had been his mother.

She'd constantly nagged and mentally bullied him until he snapped. He'd been making her some food at the time, steak and chips, and she was sat in the wheelchair at the table banging her steak knife and fork together, yelling at him to hurry up.

She'd been on at him all that day and this was the final straw. Clive was so annoyed that he stormed into the room, grabbed the knife from her and thrust it into her throat. Once he'd done it, he froze for a moment to absorb the enormity of his reaction. He tried to stop the bleeding but the more he pressed on her gaping neck with the napkin, the more her warm blood pumped out, spraying him in the face. It had gotten into his eyes and he was having difficulty seeing where the wound actually was. By the time he'd run to the kitchen, washed his face and returned, she was dead as a door nail.

He was so racked with guilt and confusion that he decided not to tell the police and instead, he had waited patiently until the blood had congealed before cleaning both her and the house up. He had even gone to the trouble of sewing her throat back together again as carefully as he could, going through her cotton collection until he found the closest match to her skin colour. He couldn't bear what he'd done, so decided to treat her as if she was still alive; live his life the way she would have wanted him to and generally do his best by her.

Everything had gone smoothly until the day the gas man came around to read the meter. He had started snooping around whilst Clive made him a cup of tea in the kitchen. He had wandered into the living room and found the old dear rotting in her wheelchair, so Clive had had to dispose of him, too. This had been a much more difficult battle. Stabbing a wheelchair-bound, frail old lady in the neck was easy, but trying to beat someone nearly twice his size with a hammer had proved a real physical test. He thought he'd lose for sure, but as they wrestled around on the floor he got in a lucky blow with the claw end. It stuck fast into the gas man's skull.

Clive couldn't help but giggle as the hammer sunk into his brain; he looked so funny, shaking around on the floor and screaming, he almost looked as if he were break-dancing. Once Clive was sure the gas man was dead, he simply dragged him into the airing cupboard and left him there. He was a smelly one. Clive was pretty certain it was probably him that was stinking the house out.

Then, a few weeks ago, there was Ding. She had called at his house offering religious comfort and salvation. She soon changed her tune once she saw his mum's corpse sat in front of the TV with pink cotton holding her throat together like a sick bow-tie. Clive didn't know her real name; he called her Ding because that's the sound the spade made when it smashed into her face. She was upstairs in the spare room.

He felt guilty by this time and decided it was probably time to do something nice for his mother, so two weeks ago, after the incident at the club, he didn't share a cab home with Rizwan. Instead, he told him he'd decided to walk. He waited outside the club for Lisa to come out and apologised to her for the incident that had occurred earlier that evening. After a while, he managed to talk her into coming back to his house and suffocated her with a plastic bag more or less as soon as she'd wheeled through the door. That bitch caused him no end of problems; it took him hours to drag her up the stairs. She was in his wardrobe.

He didn't care too much that he'd killed Lisa; he'd instantly taken a shine to her wheelchair. His mother had always wanted an electric one so that she didn't have to pull herself around everywhere. The thing was, though, as soon as he dropped her into it, her mouth drooped at either side; like she was whingeing that the chair wasn't good enough for her, from beyond the grave. He decided at that point to stop bothering about what she thought and live his life the way he wanted to live it. He even went to the pictures and considered leaving her body there but, in the end, decided it was probably better to come up with a more subtle way of getting rid of it.

After Lisa, he'd made a vow to himself never to kill again, under any circumstances, yet here he was two weeks later trying to find somewhere to stash his latest victim. The cellar was full so that was out of the question. He'd just have to stick her in his mum's room. Fucking miserable old dead bitch, served her right.

Rizwan, Jerry and Tarquin were taking an E whilst polishing off their last beers of the evening. Jerry felt an urge to go to Chameleon but he knew Tarquin wouldn't go with him and Rizwan was unlikely to bother if Clive was otherwise engaged. As Jerry's thoughts turned to Clive, he wondered how the greasy fucking weirdo had got on with his date and if he'd finally got to pop his cherry.

Tarquin was also curious as to how Clive's evening with Doreen was going; hopefully, this would be the last night he'd have to bother socialising with this lot. He was tempted to text or call her but didn't see any point in risking blowing her cover this late into the proceedings. He was also looking forward to the surprise he had in store for Rizwan in a little while. No matter how much he liked the guy, he couldn't live with himself if it ever got out to anybody who mattered that he'd been socialising with a fucking Asian. In his mind he hadn't started out as a racist;

it was a severe and unprovoked beating by a bunch of Asians that had made him that way.

Rizwan was trying to straighten his head out for the drive home. He urged them to finish off their pints quick and the three of them staggered out to the car park. As they got into the car and snaked off down the road, neither Jerry nor Rizwan noticed the police car waiting at the side of the road. Tarquin did, though, and as he heard the siren he couldn't help but smile. The tip-off had worked, that would do nicely; the fucker would end up behind bars this time for sure.

CHAPTER NINETEEN

FRIDAY 29th June - 11 p.m.

Once they'd been escorted back to Jerry's, Tarquin couldn't simply leave; it would have seemed too out of character. Plus he knew that Jerry had some more pills and some coke at home and felt like getting completely off his tits so that his mind would stop ticking over about how Doreen's night was progressing.

Rizwan couldn't believe it; caught for a second time in about as many months. He'd lose his licence and worse this time, for certain. He also felt the need to get wankered, because if he ended up in prison because of tonight's stupidity he might not get the chance again for a while.

All of them were already well on their way to mongdom thanks to the pills they'd necked just before leaving *The Nobody*. They'd done well not to let it show too much to the police. If they'd been sprung, it wouldn't have been much fun sitting alone in an empty police cell off their rockers.

Jerry got them a beer each from the fridge and they all washed another pill down with their first mouthful. As it caught the back of Jerry's throat, it made him feel gippy; if he didn't have something to line his stomach with, he knew he'd be sick. 'Somebody make me some food!'

'Fucking hell!' screamed Tarquin. 'That's disgusting. How can you eat when you've done pills?'

Rizwan didn't notice what was going on, he was quietly gurning in the corner, lost in his own little world. The group had a name for the state he was in; he was all over the chip shop. Tarquin pointed over at him and asked Jerry, 'Why don't you get him to bring you a fish back?'

Jerry managed a smile, but explained to Tarquin why he needed food so badly and told him there was a micro-wave chicken curry in the freezer. Tarquin giggled as he examined the Weight-Watchers meal. The ten minutes it would take to cook would give him and Jerry a little time to partake in a drinking game with the absinthe he'd found stashed in there.

Tarquin popped the curry into the microwave and took a pint glass from the draining board. He filled it with the absinthe which had a gloopy consistency due to the freez-ing process. He liked it that way; it went down with less burn. He grabbed the full glass and went back into the living room, 'Get the shocking roulette out, Jerry.'

Shocking roulette was a simple drinking game. It consisted of a small disk with four finger holes. Once you'd got your fingers in, you pushed a button on the top and a few seconds later the machine randomly sent a small electronic pulse to one of the holes, giving its recipient a small electric shock. That meant they were the loser and had to take a swig of the drink. As there were only two of them playing, they'd each have to put two fingers in, which would give them only a fifty-fifty chance.

'Bollocks, Tarquin! Wait until I've had something to eat.'

'Shut up, Jerry, I'm the only fucking poof in here. You're not going to be out-partied by a poof are you?' Of course he fucking wasn't. Tarquin knew just how to manipulate Jerry and took great delight in his achievement as Jerry produced the device from a drawer in his coffee table.

They placed their fingers in the holes and Tarquin pressed the button on top with his chin before jumping up and yelling, 'Aaargh!' He picked up the pint glass and took a large swig. It stung as it hit his throat, and he leaned over to catch his breath. He had to wait a good few minutes before he tried again.

He lost the next two rounds and was saved from starting another by the microwave bleeping. 'I'll get it,' he said and wandered into the kitchen. Annoyed that Jerry had gotten away with not having a drink so far, he decided he'd give him a bit of an indication as to how much his throat was burning. He reached into the cupboard above the microwave and pulled out a bottle of Tabasco sauce. He removed the curry from the microwave and furiously shook the bottle over the top of it before grabbing a fork to mix it all together. That'd fucking show him. He walked back into the lounge and passed it to Jerry with a, 'There you go, mate.'

Jerry took a large forkful and shovelled it into his mouth. The claggy lining caused by the pill managed to protect him in the short term from the fire he was chewing and he swallowed it. Tarquin was irritated but as he watched Jerry's face, he realised that the practical joke hadn't failed, it was simply delayed slightly.

'Fucking hell!' Jerry screamed and jumped out of his chair, leaping around as if somebody had set fire to his feet. 'I need a drink!' he screamed. He didn't even stop to think, his gut reaction was to cool his mouth down so he grabbed the absinthe and he downed the lot, then collapsed onto the sofa and began gasping for breath, his face bright red. Then he passed out. Tarquin's amusement changed to concern in case he'd killed Jerry, but on closer inspection he found that he needn't have worried because although he was clean out, he was panting as if he'd run a marathon.

Tarquin looked over his shoulder at Rizwan who was still in the chip shop. *Well*, he thought, *these two are a bag of fun. What am I going to do now?* It didn't take him long to decide that snorting Jerry's coke would be a good start and once he'd shot the first big line up his nose, he came up with another idea to pass the time.

He chuckled quietly to himself as he picked up the shocking roulette and carefully began putting Jerry's fingers into it. Then he pressed the button. Jerry shot bolt upright and screamed before flopping straight back down and returning to his former passed out state. Tarquin rolled around the floor in hysterics; it was one of the funniest things he'd ever seen. Like a failed Frankenstein's monster. He did it a few more times before growing bored and deciding to steal another line.

Once he'd had it, his mischievous streak came back with a vengeance. Tarquin giggled to himself as he walked into the kitchen and opened the fridge. *Excellent*, he thought as he picked up an open packet of bacon and took it back through to the lounge. He'd had some fun with Jerry, now it was Rizwan's turn. Riz was obviously not a strict Muslim, with the drinking and everything, but he hated anything to do with pigs or pork. Tarquin removed the rashers from the packet and carefully placed them over Rizwan's head and face, before taking a photograph of him with his mobile phone. He then carefully removed the rashes, put them back into the packet and returned them to the fridge.

Tarquin was pleased with himself; Fucking losers. He couldn't wait to exact some revenge on Clive.

CHAPTER TWENTY

FRIDAY 6th July – 8 a.m.

Clive hadn't been out for nearly a week. A few people had come to the door but he'd ignored them. He'd called Jerry on the Monday and said there had been a family tragedy and he had to go away with his mother for a week. Jerry had been so good about it that Clive felt quite guilty for lying, but what else was there for him to say. 'Sorry Jerry, I can't come in this week because I've been on a massive killing spree and need to come up with some decent ways of getting rid of the bodies.'

He'd come up with a few different ideas, though the best one had actually come a little too late. Eating them would have worked out really well if he'd not left them to rot; he didn't have the strongest of stomachs at the best of times, he only had to smell a curry and he ended up shitting outwards rather than downwards when he went to the loo, like a flock of angry sparrows firing out of his arse.

He'd made the gas man his first priority as the smell was growing more awful by the second. It turned out that it wasn't simply the decomposition causing the pong but the fact that he'd emptied his bowels at some point during or shortly after his death; there had been flies buzzing around him for a good few days now. Clive had heard them through the door and he'd been getting concerned that if they laid eggs in there, he'd have a serious maggot infestation. He hated maggots. As he'd opened the door, the smell had whacked him around the face like a fucking sledge-hammer and Clive had involuntarily vomited all over the gas man. This ended up being a blessing in disguise as it seemed to get rid of some of the flies. Clive ran to the kitchen and fashioned a surgical mask out of a dishcloth. He realised now that all the time and patience he'd put into embalming his mother and keeping her clean had definitely been worthwhile, as the thought of what she'd have looked like now if he hadn't made his skin crawl.

He returned to the open closet and was disappointed at how little help the mask was from preventing the smell. However, he tried to reassure himself that at least it might stop any germs from getting through. He looked down at the gas man and tried to figure out the best way of moving him. He decided that dragging him by his feet would be a good option and he grasped the ankles tight, but as he did so, he felt a strange sensation around his fingers and heard a squelching sound. He tried to put it to the back of his mind. Hopefully, it was just rotten flesh, he could cope with that, but the thought of grasping maggots was just too much to deal with.

He pulled the gas man into the kitchen and began chopping some of him up into small pieces and putting them in the freezer. The hands, arms, feet and legs were simple to slice and removing his head had been pretty straightforward, but by the time it came to doing something with the torso, his hacksaw had become blunt.

He didn't really want to go meddling around with the torso too much and he decided the best thing to do would be burn it in the back garden on Sunday night along with all of his other victims' clothes. In retrospect, this turned out to be a bad idea as the wind grabbed the smoke and dragged it across the whole street. It smelled like a barbecue so he was lucky the neighbours didn't come round on the cadge. Thankfully, as it was so late, nobody noticed, but he didn't see any point in pushing his luck and trying again. He washed the dead, burned flesh off the charred bones that were left behind, then smashed them into little pieces and stashing them in his mother's bedside drawer.

He'd used a kitchen knife to hack Fatty up into manageable chunks; she seemed to be a lot less hard work than the gas man, as her body was still relatively fresh by comparison. Her soft skin sliced easily but he had to break through the bones with his hammer. He liquidised her. It took two days to finish off, carefully feeding each part into the food processor and then draining the liquid into the big vat that used to live in the back garden collecting rain water. The fat bitch almost filled it.

That was two days ago and since then, he had been too physically exhausted to do something with Ding, Doreen and his mum. Even if he had the energy, he'd run out of ideas. He'd dragged Ding into the living room earlier in the week and damn nearly had a heart attack in the process because, as he looped his arms around her shoulders and lifted her, she let out a zombie-like groan. He'd freaked and started to think he'd not done the job properly, but then he realised it must have just been air pushing its way out of her dead body and passing through the vocal chords. It stank. His mum was sat in front of the television in the posh wheelchair and Ding's naked, lifeless body was stretched across the sofa. He'd put her face down because he couldn't bear to look at the mess he'd made of her.

A loud bang came at the door and Clive could hear a muffled shout. 'Open up, Clive! I know you're fucking in there!'

That wasn't the first time somebody had knocked. He

didn't recognise the voice at all so he quietly slipped into the kitchen and began waiting for them to get bored and leave again. But this time they weren't going. The banging grew louder and fiercer. Clive began to fear that it could be the police and, as it became apparent that whoever was out there was trying to bust the door down, his fear turned into panic. He didn't know what to do.

As the door burst open, Clive looked through the open kitchen door straight down the hall. His panic changed to confusion as he saw Tarquin. He walked towards him with his head full of questions. Why was he so determined to get in? How come he was being so aggressive? Had it been him all those times earlier in the week? And how come his voice was completely different?

'Where the fuck is she?' asked Tarquin.

Pulling the makeshift surgical mask from his face and dropping it on the floor, he splurted out, 'Who? What? What are you on about? Why are you talking like that?'

'I said, where the fuck is she?' Tarquin's tone and facial expressions were quickly becoming more angry and aggressive.

'W-W-W-Who?' stammered Clive.

'You fucking well know who! Where is she?'

'*WHO?*'

Tarquin grabbed Clive by his collar and pushed him hard against the wall that separated them from the corpses locked away in the living room. 'Doreen! You fucking freak! Where is she?'

'W-W-W-What?' Clive stammered, panic-stricken. What was going on?

Tarquin's patience was beginning to wear incredibly thin and he leaned in towards Clive. Their noses collided and pressed hard together before Tarquin growled through gritted teeth, 'I swear to God if you start another sentence with the letter W I'll fucking kill you.'

Too scared to recognise the nature the threat that had just been made, Cive asked, 'What?'

This was like a red rag to a bull. Tarquin punched Clive hard in the stomach. As he let go, Clive leaned over, winded, gasping for breath. Tarquin stood waiting patiently for him to regain his composure.

'Why did you hit me?' asked Clive. Another sentence starting with the letter W. Big mistake. It was rewarded with a tough shove onto the floor and a strong kick in the ribs. Once again he struggled to breathe. 'Why are you kicking me? What have I ever done to you?' he panted.

Tarquin took a deep breath and calmed himself; Clive wouldn't be any use to him if he couldn't speak. He squatted over Clive and grabbed him by the throat. 'Listen to me and listen fucking carefully, you little prick! Doreen hasn't called me since last Friday, just before she met you to go out. So I'm going to ask you one last time. Where the fuck is she?'

Clive was confused, the thought of killing Tarquin had passed through his mind but he'd promised himself he wouldn't do it again and he wanted to stick to that promise. But why was Tarquin so interested in Doreen? They hardly even knew each other. Clive cleared his throat and asked, 'Why would Doreen be ringing you?'

Tarquin's patience had left the building. 'Clive, just tell me where she is,' he asked menacingly.

There seemed no point in lying. Clive had dug himself into such a hole that things surely couldn't get any worse than they were already, so he simply reached up, pointed up the stairs at his bedroom door and said, 'She's in there.'

The boys sat patiently watching Dave empty the fruit machine again and wondered if he'd actually grace them with any form of conversation, or just do his usual and pretend they didn't exist. All signs were pointing to the latter and they were frustrated with the whole situation. They never won on the damn machine, it was just an endless circle of piling money in, Dave emptying it, their mum bringing more pound coins. Something was going to have to give.

As Dave secured the front of the fruit machine, grabbed the cash bag and walked back up out of the cellar Bobby noticed that his routine was slightly different this time. He'd forgotten something. 'Did you hear that?' he asked.

Billy was so despondent with the whole situation that he'd barely even realised Dave had left and asked, 'What?'

Bobby glanced at his brother and a broad grin appeared on his face as he said, 'Nothing!'

My God! thought Billy, *he's completely lost the plot.* 'How exactly am I supposed to hear nothing?'

Bobby grabbed his brother by the shoulders and began giddily jumping up and down. 'Nothing. Don't you get it? Nothing! No door locking. He's left it open.' He let go of his brother and scrambled up the stairs.

Billy began to feel uneasy. He didn't feel at all comfortable about leaving and shouted, 'You're not going out there, are you?'

'Of course I'm going. We're free! This is our chance.'

'Don't leave me, Bobby. I'm scared. I don't want to go yet.'

'Come on. We might not get another chance like this one! Let's go!'

'Look, we've waited this long. We can wait a bit longer. I will go. I – I just need a little bit of time to get my head around it, that's all. We don't know what it's like up there.

Maybe we're better off down here. Please, please don't make me go?'

Bobby considered what his brother had just said. Although he completely disagreed with him, he reasoned that perhaps being in too much of a rush could blow this chance completely. If they didn't make it this time, you could bet your life they wouldn't be so careless as to leave the door unlocked again. This was the first real opportunity they'd got and it could easily be the *only* opportunity they'd get. 'OK then. We'll wait a bit, make sure there's definitely nobody outside the door,' he said. 'Plus, we're going to need some time to have a peek around up there and plan an escape route.'

Tarquin ran back down the stairs and was promptly sick all over the floor in front of Clive. 'You sick fucking bastard!' coughed Tarquin. 'I always knew there was something weird about you.'

Clive fell to his knees, held his head in his hands and began to sob. 'It was an accident Tarquin, honest. I didn't mean to do it, she was just making so much noise. I put a pillow over her face to keep her quiet and when I looked underneath she'd stopped breathing. I didn't know what to do.'

He shuffled closer to Tarquin, his knees in the pool of vomit and flung his arms around Tarquin's legs. 'You've got to help me! I don't know what to do! Everything's gone horribly wrong! Say you'll help me, Tarquin, please.'

Tarquin looked down at the pathetic broken excuse of a man clinging for dear life to his lower legs and thought for a moment. If Doreen was dead, he wouldn't have to split the cash. 'Maybe we can help each other,' he said.

Clive looked up through blurred teary eyes and said, 'What do you mean?'

'The money,' said Tarquin.

Nothing Tarquin had said today had made any sense to Clive whatsoever. 'What money?' he asked.

'Don't you fucking start with these stupid questions. Again.'

'Seriously, Tarquin. I honestly don't have the first fucking clue what you're going on about.'

'The money your mum's got hidden in this house. I want it.'

'There is no money! I promise you, absolutely nothing! I don't know what you're talking about. I'm not lying. Please don't hit me again. If I had any money I'd give it to you.'

This got Tarquin thinking. He wouldn't lie to him now, surely, he was a mess. The old bitch must have been keeping it secret, 'Where is the old bitch?' he shouted.

'Who?'

'Your fucking mum! That's who! As if she's not told you! I can't believe it. Where is she?'

'Leave her alone.'

'Fuck that, Clivey boy. If you want my help with that body upstairs you'll tell me where she is, otherwise I'll just phone the police'

'She's not going to be able to tell you anything, Tarquin. There's no point in trying!'

'I'll be the judge of that. Where is she?'

Clive sighed, dropped his head and mumbled, 'In the lounge,' raising his eyes to glance at the closed living room door. 'But you won't get any answers from her.'

Dave put the final tick on his check list and said, 'Well Shirley, one hundred percent. Perfect, not one single item out of place, shelf wrongly stacked, surface left unpolished, or bottle in wrong date order. Absolutely incredible.'

'Oh Dave, thank you.'

'Absolutely incredible that for nearly fifteen years you've always had the ability to do the job correctly and never bothered. What a waste of my fucking time! Well, at least you got it right today. That's all that matters, I suppose.'

'What time is he coming?'

'Do you never pay any fucking attention, Shirley? I've arranged for him to come this morning before we open, that way we can't fail on account of some customer messing things up. Can you imagine how much it would affect the outcome if Paul was sat in the corner with that bear?'

'Poor bugger. Imagine having to go through what he went through. It's enough to drive anyone mad.'

'No, Shirley. You're enough to drive anyone mad. How I'm still here, sane and completely normal, I don't know!'

Tarquin returned from the living room shaking his head and smiling. 'Well, it's no wonder she fucking stank! How long's she been dead? And who's the other dead lass on the sofa?'

Clive stood up, dusted the vomit chunks from his knees and replied, 'It's a long story. You don't know how good it actually feels to get it out in the open. My mum basically ruled my life and one day I just lost it. That other lass came round saying God would forgive my sins, but when she saw what I'd done she fucking freaked, so I lost it again.'

Tarquin's shock had faded and he was beginning to

find the whole situation amusingly surreal. 'You're a regular fucking Norman Bates, aren't you?' he said. 'I suppose the old saying's right. It's always the quiet ones.'

'Please help me, Tarquin. I've fucked everything up.'

'I'll help you matey, just as soon as I've got my hands on that cash.'

'There is no money! How many more times do I have to tell you? No. Fucking. Money!'

'You're wrong Clive. The old bitch has been lying to you, I heard your uncle talking in the pub and he said that the crazy old bitch had a room full of readies. Now Doreen's dead and I've been playing the faggot act for months. I'll be fucked if I'm doing it for nothing.'

All of a sudden, Clive realised what Tarquin had been going on about but he was so far off the mark it was unbelievable. 'Follow me,' he said and led him to the back of the kitchen where there was a door leading down to the cellar. He opened it slowly, revealing the contents. 'I think you misheard . . . she won a stupid competition years ago . . . it's a room full of Shreddies.'

Bollocks! Doreen was dead and he'd been acting gay for months to try and steal a fucking truck load of boxes of breakfast cereal. However, Clive had proveed to Tarquin today that he must be capable of pretty much anything. With the dirt Tarquin now had on him, he should be able to get him to do whatever he wanted. Turning back to him, he said, 'If you want my help, you'd better find a way of getting me some cash. I was banking on that money. Unless you want me to shop you to the police like I did with your mate Rizwan. Then you'll be in a fucking loony bin where you belong.'

Clive was even more confused now. 'What have you done to Rizwan?'

Tarquin sniggered and said, 'I shopped him in for drink driving. He's in court later on today, he's bound to get sent down this time and unless you want to join him, you'll find a way of getting me enough cash to get out of this shite hole of a village once and for all.'

'What do you expect me to do? I can't just make cash magically appear from thin air.'

'You can start by coming to work with me now and getting this week's lottery money. I'll think of something else afterwards.'

'What about your end of the deal? Are you going to help me with the bodies?'

'You've lived with them for a while, a bit longer won't make any difference. You can wait until I'm paid off! Now come on! Or else they won't be the only bodies rotting in this shit hole.'

As the knock came at the back door, Dave silently prayed that this year would be his year. The takings were up, the pub was cleaner than ever and his C.C.T.V. system gave him a high tech, sophisticated edge. He approached the back door of the pub's kitchen and opened it slowly. The Landlord of the Year judge looked different than Dave had imagined, he was a lot older than usual but hopefully this would go in his favor. This man looked like he had experience on his side, he wasn't some jumped-up little fast-tracked twat that had never even run a boozer, Dave could tell. He was clearly a heavy smoker as he had a yellow streak at the front of his gray slicked back hair. As he stretched out his arm to shake Dave's hand he could see the yellow build-up on his fingers as well. So he'd been right.

'How do you do?' the man said, 'My name's Albert Finney, you must be David?'

Dave shook his hand, smiling, and said, 'Just call me Dave,' as he gently pulled him into the kitchen and closed the door behind him.

'And you can call me Al.'

Excellent, thought Dave, already on shortened name terms. This should hopefully be a breeze. 'So, *Al*, what would you like to begin with?' asked Dave.

'I thought we could get the costs and profits out of the way first, then the pub inspection. Would you like to fetch me the books?' replied Al.

'We can do better than that,' said Dave, gesturing to Shirley who was busy looking busy by the freezers at the bottom end of the kitchen. 'Shirley! Would you kindly fetch me the laptop and projector?' He turned his attention back to Al. 'Can I get you a cup of tea or coffee? Or something a little stronger?'

'A cup of tea would be lovely,' said Al.

'An excellent choice, my wife knows exactly how to make the perfect cup of tea. Follow me through to the bar and I'll get us a table. I'm sure you'll be impressed with the progress we've made this year.'

As Clive and Tarquin approached Jerry's office, Tarquin was psyching himself up to get back into camp mode. As they approached Jerry's desk, he shot up out of his chair and yelled, 'What the fucking hell time do you call this? And what the fuck are you doing here? I thought you had a family crisis!'

Tarquin jumped to the rescue, so camply and flamboyantly that Clive was having difficulty grasping the situation properly. 'Well, Jerry love, it's like this. Clive's mum had one of her turns, but she seems to be better now. He phoned me up last night for a chat and I said I'd go over and speak to him this morning and see if we couldn't have a word with his mum and get her to let him come back to work. Poor old dear, she isn't half in a bad way you know. Anyway, so here he is and here I am and that's why I'm late and that's why he's here.'

'Right,' said Jerry, then stared at Clive. 'Is that right?'

'Erm . . . yeah, yes mate. That's it. That's right.' Clive tried not to look at Tarquin as he didn't want to give anything away.

'I'm not being insensitive, Clive but that old bitch has cost me more in sick days than the rest of the fucking work force put together. Isn't it about time she just hurried up and died and put you out of your fucking misery?'

Once again, Tarquin jumped to Clive's defence. 'Don't be rotten, Jerry, you should see her. She looks like death.' He had to try hard not to piss himself laughing at what he'd just said, but carried on yapping regardless. 'Anyway, Clivey boy'll make the late time up, and he'll collect the lottery money and save you a job. Won't you, Clive?'

'Yeah, yeah sure.'

Rizwan hung his head low, he knew exactly what was coming. He'd been unlucky enough to cop for the same judge a second time and the memories of his warning a few weeks ago were burned into his brain.

'Mr Rizwan you disgust me.' the Judges first words didn't do anything to make Riz feel better. 'You have no regard for your own life, or that of anybody else who dares to venture out on to the road once you've decided to have a few drinks. A car in your hands is no more than a weapon, letting you loose with your license again would be tantamount to letting a gun-waving madman back on the streets. That's how dangerous a car is in your possession. It's an accident waiting to happen. How you haven't killed anybody yet is beyond me. And the fact that you stood there and blatantly lied to me under oath last time we met, just proves to me further that you're not even fit to be walking the streets. I'm revoking your license for five years, not that I think that alone will stop you. So in addition, to give you a little time to reflect on your stupidity and carelessness, I'm sentencing you to a custodial sentence of two months with no option for early release. Now, get out of my sight and don't ever darken my courtroom again!'

'Darken?' yelled Rizwan, 'Darken? You racialist! I cannot believe in a court of law I can be racially abused, this is a joke.'

'Mr Rizwan, I think we both know what I meant.'

'Yeah. Too right. You were mocking me!'

'Please shut up, Mr Rizwan. Your voice is like nails grinding on a blackboard.'

'Oh! *Black*board!'

Martin couldn't believe the mess that had been made of Jimbob. How somebody could go to such extremes when it was obvious that Jimbob had been really making an effort to pay off the debt was beyond him. He was home and out of hospital now, at least that was something, but he couldn't do anything for himself. His hands were bundled up so much that he looked as if he was wearing a pair of huge white boxing gloves and he had a pot and boot on his left foot.

His troubles were nowhere near over, though. Maz had paid him a little visit earlier in the week and told him in no uncertain terms that the debt still stood and the clock was still ticking. Loudly. How was Jimbob supposed to raise cash in the state he was in, for fuck's sake? The only way Martin could think of to get Jimbob out of the pickle he was drowning in, was to pay Maz a visit tonight and transfer the debt and the job of dealing to himself. He despised the idea but it had to be done, there was no alternative, and one way or another he would settle that debt, get the bass and amp back and make sure that Maz wouldn't be able to fuck anybody's life up again.

Jimbob took some persuading, but no matter how strong his resistance, it only seemed to fuel Martin's insistence. By the time Martin was ready to leave, he'd done the perfect selling job on him. He was leaving with Jimbob's mobile phone and instructions that the best time to meet Maz was early on.

Albert Finney was more than impressed; never before had he seen such an immaculately presented premises and well-oiled business mechanic. The figures were impressive and, it also helped that he'd taken a little bit of a shine to Dave. 'Excellent. You and your wife have done a marvellous job

Dave, this is a beautiful public house and an impressive business. There's just one more inspection left, but if the rest of the place is anything to go by I can't see you coming second to anyone. Splendid, truly splendid.'

One more inspection? Everything had been done! Dave was confused. There was no way he could have forgotten anything; he'd been working towards this for ages. 'What other inspection? I . . . I thought that was the lot.'

'Oh Dave, don't worry. I'm sure that even unprepared, you'll pass with flying colours. It's a new addition this year. The cellar inspection.'

Dave's heart sank. *Fucking typical!* he thought grimly. It wasn't enough that he'd had Shirley's incompetence dragging his scores down for the last few years. Now the fucking kids were going to ruin it. He'd always known they were bad for business. They'd be even worse for business if Al found out they were living down there. Nobody even knew they had any children.

Al's hand grabbed the cellar door and began to open it, but Dave promptly put his back against it to close and secure it. 'No. No there must be something else I can do,' he said, removing his wallet from his back pocket.

'A bribe?' asked Al. 'That's an instant disqualification.'

A flustered Dave grabbed Al loosely by the lapels on his suit and pleaded with him. 'There must be some kind of agreement we can come to. Surely.'

Downstairs, the sound of the door swinging open then banging closed again had got the boys' attention. 'There's something strange going on today,' said Bobby, 'I can feel it. I want to go and have a look.'

'Don't leave me, I don't want to go,' said a petrified Billy.

'I'm not going to leave you. I'm just going to have a quick peek at what's going on.'

'But what if you're seen? There's obviously somebody up there! We can't risk blowing it. Let's just wait a little bit longer.'

'I'm done with waiting. I'll be careful. Just open the door slightly, have a quick gander at what's going on and come back down. Everything'll be fine, I promise.'

Billy held a hand over his face and glared through a small gap in his fingers as his brother began slowly ascending the stairs. Tentatively and silently, one step at a time. He reached the top and stopped for a moment to press his ear against the door. Silence. He looked down at his brother and gave him the thumbs-up before carefully pulling down the handle and slowly opening the door just wide enough for him to peek through.

Fucking hell! Maybe they were being protected after all. The first glimpse of normal civilized life poor Bobby got to see was his father putting an old man's cock into his mouth. Quietly, he closed the door and descended the stairs before stopping and sitting on the bottom one. His eyes were wide and staring and his jaw had dropped open.

'Bobby!' exclaimed Billy. 'What's wrong?' He hopped towards his stunned-looking brother who was completely frozen and speechless. 'Bobby! Stop it, you're scaring me.' He waved his hand in front of Bobby's face but he didn't flinch. Not even a blink. What had he seen? What up there could possibly be so bad that it sent his brother completely into shock? Billy needed to find out.

Dave swallowed hard. By the look on his face you'd think he was swallowing a football, a salty, warm, gloopy football. Al sighed with relief as Dave stood up again and said, 'Will that do?'

Billy had struggled to make it halfway up the stairs and had to hop back down again, He was unsure if he wanted to know what his brother had seen. At the foot of the stairs he tried justifying it to himself once again. Even if there was something awful up there, he'd be able to deal with it. Take it like a man, rationalise it, find a solution, crack his brother out of the trance he seemed to be in and move on. With renewed vigour, he once again began to hop up the stairs, as slowly and as silently as he could manage. He reached the door and paused. This was it. He had a sudden pang of nerves and nearly turned back around again, but managed to stop himself. *Right, just open it a little*, he thought, *a small peek just to see what's there and then back down to tell Bobby to stop being daft.* He grabbed the handle and slowly pulled the door ajar.

He only managed a glimpse but a glimpse was more than enough. Was that normal? Natural? Perhaps it was for the best that they'd seen little of their father if he could do that to a man.

CHAPTER TWENTY-TWO

FRIDAY 6th July – 5 p.m.

As Brian pulled up outside *Jonny T's Autos* its foul-mouthed owner knew this couldn't mean anything but trouble. He'd definitely pushed his luck in palming off such a weirdo with a Mondeo that used to be two Mondeos, two stolen, smashed-up, written-off Mondeos. There would be little point in trying to prove Brian wrong; he obviously knew what he was on about. There was, however, an extremely strong case for denying any knowledge of it.

As Brian disembarked from the vehicle, Jonny couldn't help but wonder if this fucking freak ever bothered changing his clothes, or if he was simply that odd that he had a collection of identical trousers and shirts hanging in his wardrobe. Probably the latter, he decided.

Brian approached Jonny. It was obvious he was extremely annoyed because, as he'd slammed the door and started storming over, his glasses were misting up. 'This car is a safety hazard!' he screamed. 'I cannot believe you could sell something so dangerous. I was giving it a valet yesterday and underneath the mats in the back foot well I found weld marks! It's cut and indeed shut!'

'Are you sure?' asked Jonny.

Brian couldn't believe his denial. 'Sure? *Sure?* I'm absolutely fucking antiperspirant! This car is knock-off, snide and highly illegal!'

'I'm sorry mate I *bollocks, twat, knacker*, bought that car from an auction in good faith, from a well respected seller. Do you mind if I take a look?'

Brian paused briefly to consider Jonny's sincerity before agreeing. Jonny strolled over to the car, opened the back doors and lifted the mat. 'I don't believe it! You're right. I've been *fucked, shit*, ripped off.'

'*You've* been ripped off? What about me? It's me that's had my life hanging in the balance for the last five weeks driving around in that death trap. Give me one good reason why I shouldn't just report this to the proper authorities.'

Shit. Jonny needed to think fast, he needed a sweetener, an offer that Brian couldn't refuse, something that would safeguard his livelihood. 'Look, if something like this gets out my business will be *fucked, twat, cunt*, ruined! I'll report my reseller to the police and as a goodwill gesture, I'll tell you what I can do for you,' he said.

'Fire away! I'm all ears.'

You're all fucking spectacles, thought Jonny as he said, 'By way of an apology, how about I get you a brand new *cunt, twat, knob*, Mondeo Ghia X?'

Brian's mouth began to salivate as he pictured the front lower grille chrome insert and the body coloured front and rear lower bumper valances. This had got his attention. The Ghia was his dream car, sure there were other better models in the Mondeo range but he wanted comfort and class, not speed. Owning this car would be an ambition realised. 'OK,' said Brian, 'OK, but as long as you definitely deal with whoever sold you this time-bomb through the proper channels.'

'Of course. You have my absolute promise on that.' he said, pausing for a moment to stop the swearing. 'I can't have my reputation compromised.'

'Excellent. Well, can I take it now?'

'Erm . . . no, sorry, it'll take me a couple of weeks to get one in but I can give you this Corsa until it arrives.'

'A Corsa! You seriously expect me, a man of my standards to hinder my ability driving around in one of those? Are you mad?'

It was the only car Jonny had on the shop front that wasn't cut and shut, he couldn't offer anything else. 'It's the best I can do, Brian, I've got buyers interested in everything else.'

CHAPTER TWENTY-THREE

FRIDAY 6th July – 9 p.m.

Tarquin felt a lot better for having got Clive to scam him the lottery cash. It wouldn't be a good idea for him to let his guard down just yet, though; he needed to push Clive along, give him a little further encouragement, see just how far he'd be willing to go to keep his filthy little secret safe and furnish Tarquin with enough cash to get out of Holme Bridge and away to sunnier climes. He had his reasons, too many to mention; the only reason he'd ended up in this shite hole in the first place was to find a way out of the country. Nobody would ever think of looking for him here and his secret was safe with Jimbob, even if he didn't know the gay extremes Tarquin had been willing to go to.

He'd arranged to go out with Clive and Jerry, for one last time hopefully. They were both upset that Rizwan would be inside for a while and felt like drowning their sorrows. Tarquin felt like celebrating, though and with Jimbob out of action he'd be safe to go to Chameleon, but they'd meet in *The Nobody* first. Why did these fucking losers kept frequenting such a crap boozer? No music, no gambling, no fuck all! They didn't even sell Seabrooks crisps. This was Yorkshire, for fuck's sake! Any pub worth its salt should sell Seabrooks. It was one of the few things he'd miss when he finally got out.

Not that he'd fancy any this evening, anyway; the acid he'd dropped half an hour before would take care of his hunger, no problem. He'd regretted it the moment he'd taken it. Taking acid was like making a serious commitment to himself that he definitely wanted to be messy and he didn't know if he was up to being in it for the long haul. Sure, the first couple of hours would be fantastic but it would only be a matter of time before he got bored with it. That was when the acid would take over. It would start laughing at him, twist his vision, his emotions and even his hearing. The worst thing was, the more he worried about it, the worse it would be. Fortunately, by the time he'd got to the pub it hadn't kicked in yet.

Martin was terrified as he stood outside Maz's office. Jimbob's hands and feet were evidence enough that the man was capable of anything – well, capable of getting somebody to do anything for him, the low-life, spineless bastard. He was also sick to the pit of his stomach at the thought of having to deal drugs to help pay off his mate's debt. He was playing the long game though; all he needed to do was get close enough to Maz to find a weakness to exploit. He'd think of something, something that would make his life and his whole seedy empire come crashing down around him.

He'd pay for threatening the success of the band. They all shared the same vision, all had the same optimistic outlook on their future success, they never said, 'If' we get a record deal or 'If' we win a brit award, it was always, 'When'. Sure, bass players were easy to find, but that didn't matter, it wasn't the noise Jimbob produced that made him indispensable, it was the magic that happened when the three of them got on stage. They'd had other people in the band before, an extra guitarist or two and a keyboard player had come and gone. They'd improved the overall sound of the band but diluted the magic. The only way they would make it would be as a threesome, that's how it felt right.

Martin knocked on the door, waited to be called and walked inside. Maz was sat at his desk with one of his thugs standing behind him and from the rolled-up note, credit card and remnants of white powder on the table, it was a pretty safe bet to assume he'd already been on the coke.

'Who the fuck are you?' he asked.

'My name's Martin. I'm a good friend of Jimbob's.' His heart was pounding so hard he thought his ribs might break under the strain.

'If you've come here looking for trouble, this guy stood behind me will gladly deliver some your way, man.'

'No. Not at all. I've come here because I want to help you.'

Maz glanced at the scrawny-looking indie kid stood in front of him, looking him up and down and asked, 'And how the fuck are you expecting to do that?'

'Well,' he said, 'Jimbob owes you money which, judging by the fucking mess you made of him, is pretty important to you that you get back.'

'And.'

'And as you are no doubt aware, he's out of commission at the moment. Not much use to anybody.'

'Yeah.'

'So what I thought was this; I could take over the work he's been doing for you for free until I've worked off his debt.'

Maz's coke-fuelled paranoia began to kick in. He stood up, banged on the desk and yelled, 'I don't even know who the fuck you are, man! Do you really think I'm that fucking stupid that I would let somebody I've never fucking met before loose in me club, working for me?'

'I can see where you're coming from, Maz but if I wanted to cause you any trouble I'd have done it. I'm not interested in fucking revenge or playing stupid games. The only thing that interests me is the well-being of my bass player. I've come here to speak to you man to man, to come to some kind of reasonable, peaceful solution to the problems he's caused you. This way we'll both get what we want. You get a dealer and your money back and I get a guarantee from you that you'll leave Jimbob alone. For good.'

This seemed to relax Maz a little and he took his seat. 'What do you mean "for good"?' he asked.

'What I mean is, the month or so it'll take me to work off Jimbob's debt is long enough for you to find somebody else to take over.'

Maz was getting irate again, Martin could see it in his eyes. 'Why the fuck should I agree to this?'

'Because, I'm the reason that Jimbob actually managed to show up here and be able to pay you anything at all last week. I bailed him out. The only person that can lose out on this deal is me if I fuck up. Which I won't.'

Maz still had a face like thunder as he pulled open his desk drawer. Martin's heart sank; he couldn't see the contents from where he was stood but there was a pretty good chance it contained the hammer which already carried the blood of Jimbob Rifkin or even worse, a gun. Maz stretched out his hand and reached into the drawer. He grabbed hold of something and then looked directly at Martin, who was now so petrified the only thing he could hear was his own heartbeat smashing hard against his ear drums.

'OK,' said Maz, 'you start now.' He pulled out a huge bag of pills and threw them across the room.

Jonny stood waiting outside Chameleon. Taking a girl clubbing was the perfect way of not having to make idle chit-chat, as long as he could get through the pleasantries he'd be fine and hopefully, by the end of the night she'd be too pissed to notice. This one was called Emily and he hoped she'd be better looking than the other bird from the Gazette two weeks before. She said she'd be wearing a vest top with Ermintrude from *Magic Roundabout* printed on the front with the word 'Moo' underneath.

After a while, he saw her. She was all right looking, good figure, dark hair, OK face. She came over and spoke. 'Jonny?' she asked, her bottom jaw wobbling all over the place.

Jonny cleared his throat and steadily said, 'Yes, you must be Emily,' Excellent. He took a small breath and followed up with, 'how are you?'

'GodI'vehadafuckingnightmareofadayactuallyfirstthing that happened was I got up this morning and my alarm hadn't goneoffsoIendeduplateforworkthenwhenIgotinmybastard boss gave me a fucking warning like it was my fault the fucking cheekytwatsoItoldhimhereI'mnotyourfuckingskivvyjustcos Iworkforyoudoesn'tgiveyoutherighttorulemylifeandhesaid well if that is how you feel why don't you just go and find a job somewhere else so I said wellI just might and he said well go on thensoIsaidokandIleftthenwhenIgotbackhomemyexboy-friendhadonlybeenroundandtakenalltheDVD'sBASTARD theywereallfuckingminenoneofthemwerehissoIthoughfuck thisandwentouttobuymyselfanewskirtfortonightdoyoulike it? nice one so yeahI don't usually come in here cos a few of my matesreckonit'sadivebutIthinkit'sallrightdoyoufancyadab ofspeed?'

As she came up for breath, Jonny realised that *his* speech problem would be the least of his worries with this crazy speed-head in tow and began planning his exit strategy. The *Gazette* had proved to be a pretty piss-poor way of meeting up with girls and he hoped the extra cash invested in the video dating would provide a better calibre of woman.

CHAPTER TWENTY-FOUR

FRIDAY 6th July – 11 p.m.

Tarquin was absolutely off his fucking rocker, the acid had really taken hold. He hadn't started visually tripping yet but it was only a matter of time; every inch of his body was tingling just like that perfect millisecond before an enormous sneeze. He was grinning like a Cheshire cat, his eyes were wide open, his fully dilated pupils moving almost independently of each other like some deranged chameleon and everything he looked at had that hazy glow around it that meant that sooner or later, it would start changing shape.

Clive was over at the bar getting some beers in. Second by second he was running out of patience with Tarquin. Every time Jerry's back had been turned he was throwing Clive evil stares and making sarcastic remarks. Thankfully, now that the acid had properly kicked in, he seemed a bit more preoccupied with trying to keep his own head straight.

Clive had decided not to bother with any chemicals this

particular evening; he had too much to worry about to be poisoning his body with that man-made shite. It would have him crying into his Shreddies come Monday morning and with all the grief he was getting at the moment, he needed control of his head.

Clive desperately wanted to confide in somebody about everything that had gone on, but who would possibly listen? People didn't tend to enjoy lending a kind ear to psychopaths. Not sympathetically, anyway, just sick curiosity and that's not what he needed, he needed somebody to realise that he had been and still was the victim in all of this. The whole situation seemed so fucked, it was beyond repair. He'd just have to grin and bear it whilst he went along with every crazy demand Tarquin could come up with until his cash lust had run out, then get his help to dispose of the bodies. Unfortunately, it wouldn't be until then that Clive could wave his entire troubles goodbye.

Jerry was pissed off. There was no point in him even bothering to try and go on the pull because the hairs on his legs were only just starting to come through and from his ankles to his balls he had thick, ginger, itchy stubble. He wished he'd thought it through properly instead of getting caught up in the moment.

He was also pissed off because Rizwan had lost his license and was banged up; it would end up costing him a fortune in taxis.

As Clive returned from the bar, Tarquin couldn't help but giggle and said, 'You look a right twat in those! When did you get them?'

Clive didn't have the first clue what he was going on about, 'What?' he asked.

'Those fucking mad glasses you've got on. You look like a right fool.'

All had become clear, he was obviously in the early stages of tripping; seeing people in glasses was a very common starting point. Clive smiled inwardly; the great thing about people on acid was how responsive they could be to a little gentle suggestion. It was time for him to have a little fun at Tarquin's expense for a change. 'It's you that looks a fool, Tarquin. Everybody except you has a pair on. Take a look around.'

As Tarquin scanned the club, he could see that Clive had been absolutely one hundred percent correct; every single person in the entire club was wearing those ridiculous-looking Dame Edna Everidge glasses. The barmen, the clubbers, the bouncers, shit, even the fucking D.J. had them on. Was there some sort of dress code he'd not been informed of? Had there suddenly been a new fashion trend he'd missed? Why were people pointing at him and laughing? Then, as his vision steadied and he recognised the people laughing to be Clive and Jerry, he suddenly realised what had been going on.

'You fucking bastards!' said Tarquin as he hung his head in his hands. He knew better than to try and fight it though, any attempt to iron out his brain would only end up putting more creases in it. He was going to need a little chemical help and decided that having a couple of pills would lighten his mood, stop him from getting too tired and prevent things from turning nasty. Unfortunately, with Jimbob stuck at home he didn't know where to get any from and he couldn't just go wandering around in the state he was in asking random people. Then he remembered seeing the lead singer from Jimbob's band kicking around earlier on and decided to find him; maybe he'd know where to get some.

Tarquin slowly lifted his head and was relieved to see that none of the clubbers were wearing glasses anymore. This would probably be his last chance. 'I'm off to get some pills, who wants some?' he asked.

'Not for me,' said Clive, 'I'll stick to the booze.'

'Go on then,' said Jerry, 'I'll have a couple, here's a tenner.'

'Right then, see you in a bit,' said Tarquin, standing up and trying to compose himself.

Jerry was sniggering as he watched Tarquin's attempt at looking sober. He looked a real mess. 'Good luck, mate!' he said.

Tarquin didn't hear Jerry's well-wishes as he was off

like a shot. He wanted to get this over with as quickly as possible. He stumbled across the club like the fastest tightrope walker in the west, arms swinging all over the place as he tried to maintain his balance. Fortunately he was in sync with the music, so rather than looking like a complete tool, he just looked like a bit of a prick.

Martin was at the bottom corner of the club next to a machine that dispensed bottles of Bud, Volvic or Miller light for three pounds a pop. It was a quiet night; he'd chosen this spot as there was usually a healthy queue of punters lined up rolling their cash in. Sooner or later, everybody that came in would visit this machine rather than hanging around for ages at the bar. Tonight was too quiet, though. It would take him ages to pay off the debt if the club stayed this empty. He decided it was probably best to try and push the coke a bit, as one bag of that would pay the equivalent of five pills.

Somebody was stumbling towards him. He recognised the face but couldn't remember where from. The guy looked absolutely off his head. He'd clearly had enough of whatever it was he was having.

'All right, mate?' said Tarquin. 'You're in Jimbob's band, aren't you?'

Jimbob's Band? What the fuck did he go around telling people when Martin wasn't around? 'Erm. Yeah. I'm Martin, how are you doing?'

'Not bad, mate. Not bad at all.' He glanced around to make sure Jerry wasn't anywhere near before completely dropping the campness in his voice. 'Do you know who's looking after things whilst he's stuck at home?'

Who the fuck was this guy and how did he know so much? 'I'm doing it actually. How do you know Jimbob then?'

'Oh, God! You could write an entire fucking book on how long that story is, mate, we go way back. Can I have four splats, please?'

'Erm . . . yeah, course you can. Twenty quid. Do you fancy some coke? I've got some dynamite stuff here, fifty quid?'

'Fuck it, why not! In for a penny in for a pound, eh?' Tarquin was trying to conserve the lottery money but a bit of coke would probably work out nicely. He handed the cash over to Martin and set off back towards Clive and Jerry.

Martin was worried about the state that poor bloke would end up in after consuming all the narcotics he'd just supplied him. He felt a little guilty for selling him the coke but, if he was as good a friend of Jimbob as he made out he was, then surely he wouldn't mind paying the few quid extra to help bail him out.

Tarquin gave Jerry his pills and they both washed one down with their now warm beer. Tarquin considered offering the other two a line of coke but thought, *bollocks to it* and went to the toilet on his own.

He lowered the lid and removed the bag of cocaine from his pocket before emptying an unhealthily large amount on to the closed toilet seat.

A bang came at the door. 'Fucking hurry up!'

'Won't be a minute,' said Tarquin, frantically chopping and lining up his coke.

He'd rushed it; the line was a little lumpy but it would have to do. He put the bag back into his pocket and pulled out a ten pound note which he began rolling. As he did, a bouncer popped his head over the top of the cubicle. He was wearing those stupid fucking glasses and could see exactly what mischief Tarquin was up to.

'Hurry up, mate! There's other people want a turn!'

As Tarquin snorted the line, he realised there was another reason for Chameleons popularity; the bouncers didn't give a fuck about you taking drugs as long as you didn't make a twat of yourself.

After a while of waiting around outside the loos, Clive had convinced Jerry to leave. Tarquin was so wasted he didn't even notice, he just walked to the bar, ordered a beer from a bespectacled bar-maid and headed off to the safe haven and comfort of the chill-out room.

He staggered up the dimly lit backstairs and pushed open the door at the top, that was better, a bit more bright and airy. He took a deep breath at the less polluted air and allowed the ambience to sink into his brain as he navigated his way passed the pool table, across the bar and eventually flopped down onto one of the plush leather couches in the corner. He wanted the effect of the pill to take hold, but the coke seemed to be suppressing it, and the alcohol. He was left in the one state he didn't want to be in; feeling the full, undiluted effect of the acid. He slouched back and glanced around the room, then something caught his eye.

It was a small lamp at the side of the bar. He'd seen it before, loads of times, but tonight it looked different, he could see the heat waves it was giving out and they were red. *This isn't so bad*, he thought, *maybe everything will be fine after all.* As he concentrated on the lamp it slowly began to change. It was becoming more angular, like a hexagon shape and taller, it was stretching, and were those small mirrors at the top of it? Then it dawned on him what it had turned into and he began laughing hysterically. He couldn't believe what he was seeing, it was a fucking glasses rack. Not just a simple glasses rack though, as it began slowly rotating and then flying out into the middle of the room. Every time he blinked, the rack returned to its original place, then he realised if he blinked in time with the music he had control over it. It was his own personal light show.

People were looking at him and staring. It was probably

not the best idea to be laughing his head off, blinking in time with the music whilst sat alone in the corner of the chill-out room. He blinked furiously a few times until the lamp returned to its normal state, then he began to glance around again. Near the exit he could see an ornamental bust stood on an attractive marble stand. It must have been new, he'd certainly not seen it before. As he tried to figure out who the bust was of somebody knocked it on their way out of the club. It began to wobble and looked like it might fall of its stand. Tarquin leaped into action, ran across the room and grabbed it with both hands to secure it. *Phew, that was close*, he thought and as he turned his head, he spotted a room full of people all giggling and pointing at him.

What was so funny? He'd just stopped an expensive ornament from smashing into pieces all over the floor. Then, as Tarquin turned his head back around, he realised it hadn't been a bust at all, and he still had a good firm grip on it; it was the face of a very angry looking bouncer.

'I think it's time for you to go home mate.' *No shit*, thought Tarquin as he left the club in search of a cab.

Once he'd arrived home, Tarquin went straight upstairs to his bedroom. He looked at himself in the mirror on the wall to check his eyes and was distressed to see how dry his skin looked. Then it slowly began to peel and flake off.

Fuck this, he thought as he flopped down onto his bed. He prayed for sleep to arrive as soon as possible. He wished he had some Temazepam, even some fucking Nytol would do. The images flashing above on the ceiling were like a slideshow of his childhood, a bunch of memories he'd rather forget. He closed his eyes tightly, only to see haunting images of Clive's mum and Doreen.

Whilst all this had been going on, he had a single word buzzing around in his brain; 'Chandrion.' What did it mean? Was it even a word? It was now, he thought, that's the word that describes the state you're in when acid is laughing at you. He'd learned his lesson, he was too old and complex for acid. He decided that no matter how much it felt like a good idea, he'd never take another tab or munch another mushroom. No way, under any circumstances would he ever let acid chandrion him again.

CHAPTER TWENTY-FIVE

FRIDAY 13th July – 8 a.m.

The Nobody Inn had seen more than its fair share of controversy in its early years. Dave wasn't the first Landlord to live there who had a screw loose, by any means. The pub used to be called the *Wishing Well* back in the eighteen hundreds, due rather appropriately to the old dried-up well that stood in the centre of what was now the car park. The original landlord was also very precious about his premises but took his obsession to slightly more sinister extremes than Dave had done; if anybody dared complain about anything, they ended up in small pieces at the bottom of the well.

The idiot ended up getting caught and was hung for his sins. After this, the Inn had stayed empty for years. The guy who finally bought it filled in the well and tried to rebuild the business. He had little success at first because of the stigma attached to the building, but, to make the point clear that the place was free from its murky past, he changed the name to 'The No Bodies Inn'. Soon, people started to come back out of sheer curiosity. Over the years, locally the pub ended up being referred to as 'The Nobody'. It was Dave who adjusted the name to its current form when he moved in. And today Dave was going to end up with one more thing in common with the Landlord who opened the Wishing Well all those years ago; he was going to get caught.

Martin couldn't believe the mess he'd managed to get himself into; or rather, Jimbob had got him into. It'd been a hectic, stressful, horrible week and today was easily the worst day of them all. Life had pushed him in the mud and kicked him in the bollocks.

First off, there had been the whole Maz situation the previous Friday. He was lucky to walk out of that with his limbs intact and had never been as scared in his life. To add insult to injury, the club had been particularly quiet over the weekend and he'd only managed to get enough cash together to stump up a fifth of the cash that Jimbob owed, not that it mattered now. Martin ended up having to trundle home with hundreds of pills and loads of coke. It wouldn't have been so bad if he could drive. Maybe then he could have done some deliveries throughout the week and what happened on Monday might have been prevented.

Whilst he'd been over at Jimbob's house making sure he was all right, things had been afoot over at his place. It was being burgled, completely ransacked. They'd taken everything that was easy to grab; cd's, X-Box games, his cheque book, the cash and of course the massive bag of drugs in his bedroom. The twat that had done it had even left a note explaining how sorry he was and that he had no choice but to do it. Fucking smack-head bastards! Of course they had a choice! Don't take fucking heroin in the first place, you fucking losers! Martin felt extremely strongly about it. People on his street got burgled by people trying to feed their habits all the time. Unfortunately for him, it wasn't as if he could even report it to the police because, even if they managed to catch whoever was responsible, it would only leave a massive drug trail leading straight back to him.

The whole situation left him in a real pickle; no cash to pay Maz, no drugs to give back and not even enough money to pay for the repair of his window. He was supposed to be at Chameleon at nine to pay up and report for duty, but plans had had to change.

At Jimbob's on the Tuesday, Martin had to break the news about what had happened. Whilst he was there, Jimbob received a call from an old friend of his named

Tarquin, Jimbob was being really defensive about how they knew each other, but did inform Martin that Tarquin had called asking if Jimbob knew how to get hold of a gun.

Shirley sat down in the office to watch Al's pub inspection, Dave hadn't said a bad word to her all week and she couldn't quite believe that she'd manage to get away with him not complaining about a single thing. She wanted to check and make sure for herself that the inspection had gone as perfectly as she'd been led to believe but, as the tape progressed, her emotions went from complete satisfaction at a job well done to sheer horror and disgust. How could Dave betray her trust in such an intimate fashion? With a man! A fucking ugly old man! This was it, this was the final straw. The final kick up the arse she needed to put the wheels in motion for the exit plan.

She'd lived in fear of him for too long and had allowed herself to become a victim, more or less allowed herself to believe all the nonsense he threw at her. No more! She held her head in her hands and sobbed as quietly as she could to make sure he couldn't hear her and thought about what she'd let happen to the children over the years.

He'd kept her locked upstairs for the whole duration of

her pregnancy, insisting he knew best, telling the regulars she'd gone to visit a sick relative. He even delivered the babies himself, but when they were born he freaked. He blamed Shirley for their disfigurement. She tried to explain that if he'd let her go to the hospital, they perhaps could have done something. This fell on deaf ears. Dave insisted he could do something and made Shirley assist as he separated them himself.

Bobby was the healthier of the two, he had all of his limbs intact, but Billy was fused to his brother's back ribs just under the shoulder blade. He had one good arm and one good leg on his right side and a small useless claw of a foot on his left. He had no left arm due to where he was connected to his brother.

She'd had to hold back tears every week as she washed them, looking at the ugly scars that had been left behind from Dave's DIY surgery.

Clive sat in his room thinking. At least today it would all be over one way or another, he'd either be dead, in prison, or completely in the clear. Whatever the outcome, he'd be out of the whole sticky mess he'd got himself into once and for all.

Things started to go even more wrong on the Saturday

when five of the numbers that popped out of the lottery machine that night should have given the S-Packers work-force an equal share in a seven thousand pound purse. That was if Tarquin hadn't stolen the ticket money. They couldn't believe their bad luck. It was like a recurring nightmare. At least last time the entire company had been partly responsible, nobody had reminded Jerry to collect the money after all. This time the money had been collected and they would have to come up with the winnings some-how. A plan was needed and fast. They'd had a heated conversation about getting a possible solution to the situ-ation and Tarquin had come up with a few ideas. Even though Jerry hadn't had anything to do with the cash going missing that particular week, Tarquin had convinced him that they were all jointly responsible, and he'd told Jerry that it was as much his fault as Clive's because there'd been plenty of occasions in the past when Jerry had spent it. Eventually he'd caved in and agreed to do what-ever it was that needed doing to resolve the situation. Not that either of them knew at this stage what it would involve.

Tarquin had told them they'd discuss it further when they got to work later on. He told them he had everything arranged except for a few minor details. Jerry had had to arrange them a half day off work, telling the head honcho they were going to pick up the lottery money.

Clive was fed up with playing games and hoped this time Tarquin wouldn't rip them off and be in it simply to benefit himself. His first idea had been to force Clive to rob the new dealer from Chameleon to cover the amount they owed, but once Clive had gone through with it and given the stash over, Tarquin just laughed and snatched everything from Clive, amazed that he'd actually gone through with it. Clive had felt so guilty about what he had done that he'd even written a note apologising. He was relieved that he'd never met the guy as that would have just made him feel even worse.

This was it! Tarquin would finally have enough cash to get away once and for all. With all but a couple of jobs left to do everything was looking rosy, for once.

He'd enjoyed this week so far. He was finally putting the last few pieces in his escape puzzle and the end of his traumatic journey was so close he could smell it. The light at the end of what had been an extremely long and dark tunnel was coming thick and fast. He thought it would be a nightmare shifting the bag of drugs Clive had stolen for him, but after a while of touting it around and getting no response, some bloke had phoned him out of the blue and said he was interested. He had to meet him at a café in town later on. Finally, for once in his life things actually seemed to be going his way.

Shirley had made herself a 'things to do' list, just one last list, one last schedule and that would be the end of it.

1. Speak to the brewery and arrange a good deal on the quick sale of the pub.
2. Open a personal account and transfer all the funds from the business into it.
3. Put the tape somewhere safe.
4. Deal with Dave.
5. Get the kids and go.

A simple five point plan and then it would all be over. It would definitely be the best for everyone concerned. Her, the children and the brewery; they would definitely be happy, they'd been trying to get their hands on Dave's little empire for years.

Shirley and the kids certainly deserved a reward in return for what they'd had to endure. She thought that the money the business had made would be the least he could do; after all, it had been her hard work blood sweat and bucket load of tears that had made the place a success.

She'd turned a poky village pub into a regular little

goldmine and could expect at least four hundred and fifty grand for the sale of the business and the building. That, combined with the savings they'd made by tucking the bulk of the profits away over the years, would take the total to well over half a million. That should easily be enough. Dave had stupidly left himself wide open and Shirley was annoyed at herself for not thinking of doing it before. It was so unbelievably simple; he'd signed the responsibility for everything over to her including the books and the banking; she had the authority to do anything she liked with the finances.

CHAPTER TWENTY-SIX

FRIDAY 13th July – 11 a.m.

'Right, then,' said Tarquin. 'It's all just about sorted. It's simple, as far as work is concerned, we should be back here for six o'clock with the cash and they needn't ever be any the wiser.'

'What exactly have you got planned for us?' asked Jerry.

Tarquin sighed and rubbed his eyes, 'Do you want the short answer or the long answer?'

'Short!'

There didn't seem any point in sugar coating anything, 'Right, well . . . we're going to do a robbery.'

Clive and Jerry were absolutely speechless, they didn't know the first thing about any of this. They were, however, aware of the possible outcomes. Firstly, if they didn't do something they'd end up in jail and hated by the entire village for taking the lottery syndicate money. Secondly, if they did go through with this ridiculously obscene idea and got caught, the repercussions would be far worse, a long term stretch in prison wouldn't be kind to fresh meat like them. Thirdly, if they were crazy enough to go through with it and everything went smoothly all of their problems would be over. It was a gamble.

Here was the situation; Tarquin would be doing it with or without Jerry, which basically meant that Clive would have no option but to do it anyway. For Jerry the odds were long but the rewards were massive and if there was one thing Jerry had a weakness for, it was long odds with massive rewards. He loved to gamble. Unfortunately, at the moment the odds were still a little too high even for a bloke as mad as him to take a chance on. He needed some further reassurance to help make his mind up and said, 'We don't have a clue about doing a robbery. How do you seriously expect us to pull it off?'

Again, Tarquin thought there seemed little point in deceiving them. 'I don't know yet.'

Tarquin could see his response hadn't done much to build further confidence in the plan. He was going to have to let them know he'd involved somebody else in it sooner or later and decided he could use it as a good way of building some faith in the project, 'but I've managed to get somebody else on board. A professional, plenty of experience, done this thing before and he reckons he can execute the whole thing without implicating any of us. Think about it, the chances of us getting caught are pretty slim, we'll disguise our faces. None of us have had a run-in with the police before, they won't have our prints or D.N.A. to match up and they'll definitely have a suspect list as long as their arms for a job like this one.'

The fact that *a professional* was involved made Jerry's mind up but he had an idea. 'There's got to be a smarter way of doing things,' he said.

'Well, if you can come up with something better, Jerry,' Tarquin retorted.

'Maybe I can.'

Fuck! That was all Tarquin needed, Jerry sticking his bastard oar in and pissing about with the plan at this late juncture. 'Let's have it then, Jerry. Let's listen to what you've come up with that'll be so much better,' Tarquin said sarcastically.

'Well, down south this guy walked into a Blockbuster video in a posh suit and asked to speak to the manager, the fellow behind the counter said he wasn't in. This guy tells them he's from head office and needs to check the back office, like an audit or something, so one of the staff shows him to the room. Anyway, he's in there for about ten minutes before he comes steaming out, lines all the staff up and starts fucking screaming at them about what a fuck-up everything is and how he can't believe the store's being run so badly. He tells them all to fuck off for an early lunch while he closes the store for an hour and sorts the problem out. So, these dense fuckers all piss off with their tails between their legs for some lunch, all the time shitting themselves that they're going to get sacked. As soon as they've gone, this guy piles all the money and as many recent DVD's and games as he can get his hands on, fills up a transit van and fucks off.'

'Never,' said Clive.

'Serious,' Jerry added 'and that's not the best bit, these guys get back from lunch and they're so fucking stupid that it's two hours before they even notice loads of stuff has gone missing. They think he must have tidied it away.'

'You're fucking joking?'

'Here, it gets fucking better, once they figure it out, they're shitting themselves that much it takes them another fucking hour to call the police. By the time anyone knew about it, the guy was gone with thousands of pounds worth of kit. He could have got to the arse end of France with everything by the time the police got there.'

Clive was enthralled, but Tarquin was less amused. He began slowly clapping like a cheerleader applauding a geek at the end of an American teen flick. 'Brilliant,' he said, 'Fucking brilliant. That's your plan, is it?'

'I thought it was pretty good,' said Clive.

'Fuck off, Clive, it's bollocks!' snapped Tarquin, 'For one thing, everyone round here knows everyone. Christ! Rizwan's fucking cousin works in Blockbuster, you tool.'

Clive knew better than to push it, it was obvious Tarquin had a very clear idea of what he wanted to do. He thought he'd best interject and get the conversation back to the job in hand. 'OK, point taken. But we don't know this *professional* from Adam. What's in it for this mystery bloke?'

'None of that's important, all that matters is, he's got a plan and he'll let us take the amount we need for the lottery syndicate, on the proviso that he gets the rest of the cash,' lied Tarquin.

Clive knew this would definitely be bullshit; there was no way Tarquin would be involved in this just to sort the lottery cash out. He was obviously getting a larger cut. But it sounded fair to Jerry, he didn't know any better and said, 'You told us there were a couple of minor details that need sorting.'

'Yeah, just two things. We need some stockings for our heads and a driver.'

'I'll get the stockings.' Jerry blurted almost instantly.

'Well, where the fuck am I supposed to find a driver?' asked Clive.

'You're a resourceful and well connected chap, Clive,' said Tarquin 'I'm sure you'll think of something.'

Shirley had feigned illness and Dave was busy working downstairs for a change. She giggled as she watched him on the monitors struggling to get everything finished before the doors needed opening. *Fucking wanker*, she thought as she picked up the phone to call the solicitors. She'd arranged the deal on the pub and got the full asking price from the brewery, she just needed to make an appointment to see a solicitor so she could sign all the paperwork. After replacing the receiver, she popped the video tape into the envelope she'd prepared for it.

All the wheels were in motion; unbeknown to Dave, by the end of the day he'd have nothing but the cash in the till. She pressed the intercom button on the monitor console to communicate with her ear piece. Dave was wearing it today and as he heard it crackle he looked into one of the cameras. Shirley creased her nose in disgust, stared straight into his eyes on the monitor and calmly said, 'I've managed to get a doctor's appointment so I'm going out, do you need anything whilst I'm gone?'

Dave shook his head and Shirley grabbed everything she needed, the video, the contents of the safe and her handbag. She took a deep breath and tried not to think about what would be the most difficult part of the plan once she got back. Telling him.

CHAPTER TWENTY-SEVEN

FRIDAY 13th July – 1 p.m.

Maz wasn't about to meet some guy he'd never dealt with to go and do a drug deal, that would be stupid. It would be a lot more stupid to let somebody else get their hands on them though. As soon as it got back to him that somebody was punting around a few hundred pills and some already bagged-up coke, the alarm bells started ringing. Had that fucking mate of Jimbob's fucked him over? Either way, there was no way he'd let anybody else get their hands on them. The way he figured it, he was in a win win situation; even if they were the ones he'd given Martin to sell, he'd just buy them back at less than cost, make Martin take on the re-sale value as a debt and then sell these on at full price again, doubling his money. He'd already made arrangements to meet Martin at Chameleon in a couple of hours. He didn't think he'd show up but he wouldn't be able to hide; if he ran away he wouldn't be stupid enough to leave Jimbob behind and it would be easy to trace a guy with bandaged hands and feet.

Maz decided to send Mick along, one of his bouncers, much to Mick's annoyance. He was really starting to get fed up with doing Maz's dirty work, it had been bad enough having to smash Jimbob's fingers and toes up, but sending him to go on a drug deal was a step too far. Not that he had any choice. Maz had given him a grand in cash and instructed him not to pay more than a pound a pill and thirty pounds for a gram of coke. Mick was sat waiting with a mug of coffee and a greasy bacon sandwich. The bloke he was meeting should know who he was looking for in the café; there weren't that many six and a half foot meat heads in Holme Bridge and he'd been given a description.

It wasn't long before Tarquin turned up. He ordered himself a cup of tea and some crisps, sat down across from Mick and said, 'Hello.'

Mick was amused to see that it was the same bloke that he'd thrown out of the club a week earlier for holding his face; at least he couldn't be a cop. No policeman would get in that much of a state. 'What have you got for me?' he asked.

Tarquin recognised the bloke as one of the bouncers from Chameleon but couldn't remember their encounter the previous week. He was surprised how forward this guy was, but he wasn't bothered, they both clearly wanted this over with as quickly as possible. Tarquin knew idly talking about pills and coke in a café wasn't a good idea and knew he'd have to use some sort of code, 'I've got two hundred and eight of the little ones and fifteen of the other.'

How subtle, thought Mick. 'On you?'

'Yeah,' said Tarquin. As he placed the rucksack he'd been carrying on the floor, he kept tight hold of it. No way was he letting this bruiser grab them and run.

'I'll give you fifty pence a piece for the little ones and two hundred for the rest.'

'Fuck that. I know you need to make a profit but it costs more than fucking fifty pence for a king size Mars bar. You're having a laugh.'

Mick glanced at Tarquin and scowled. 'Do I look like I'm fucking laughing?'

He certainly didn't. He looked very far from laughing. Tarquin didn't know what to say, he'd obviously pissed him off.

'What were you expecting?' asked Mick.

'I don't know. A couple of grand?'

Mick couldn't be bothered haggling anymore and decided it wouldn't be safe to sit around in the café counting through the money to make sure Maz got his price. He'd just offer the grand, do the deal and get the fuck out.

'You're living on another fucking planet mate. But it's your lucky day, because I haven't got the patience or the time to fuck around. So you're going to take this thousand I'm offering you and then I'm going to walk outside with that bag, you're going to sit here, eat this sandwich, finish off your tea and walk outside. If what's in this bag is what you say it is you'll be able to stroll home and forget this ever happened. But if you've fucked me over you'll be walking into a fucking early grave. Do we have a deal?'

Tarquin sat quietly for a moment. There seemed little point in pissing this guy off any further, especially considering he'd be getting a shit load of cash from the robbery later on, and agreed. Mick passed him an envelope under the table, which Tarquin slyly checked before pushing the bag over slowly with his foot.

Mick grabbed it, calmly left and examined the contents of the bag as he walked around the corner to Chameleon. Everything seemed to be in order. Once he'd got inside the club and up to the office, he passed the stash over to Maz who examined them for a few seconds. They were definitely his drugs. Silly little cunt.

As Clive approached *Jonny T's* he wondered how to properly broach the subject with him. There would be no point in telling the truth; it would only serve to open up the floodgates for a load more trouble. He'd definitely have to make up some bullshit story and hope for the best. Fingers crossed, by the time he realised what exactly was going on he'd be too deep into it to back out. It would be hard to say no when a bunch of guys piled into the back of the car with a bag of money and a gun.

He'd just returned from making a phone call in his office when he greeted Clive on the forecourt and whoever had been on the other end of the phone had obviously been delivering good news as Jonny looked extremely pleased with himself.

'Now then, Clive, business or pleasure?' he said, rubbing his hands together as if a deal was imminent.

'Erm . . . business.'

Excellent, thought Jonny, today just keeps on getting better. 'Passed your test, have we? I've got some lovely *shit, twat, fucker*, run-arounds I can do you a good deal on.'

'No, no, no. Not that sort of business.'

What other sort of business was there? This was a fucking car lot after all. What was Clive up to? 'Eh?'

'Well, the thing is you see, we need to pick some cash

up from the bank. For work. It's erm, the lottery cash, the syndicate won! So we need somebody to give us a lift and pick the cash up.' Clive was amazed he'd managed to get through saying his lie without letting anything slip.

'What about that mate of yours, that Rizwan, can't he do it?'

'No, he's in fucking prison. He got done for drink driving again.'

'Shit! Well yes then, I'll do it what the *fuck, twat, knacker*, fuck. When do you want me?'

'We're all going to meet in *The Nobody* at four.'

'Ah, well, that poses a little bit of a problem for me then, I'm afraid.'

'Why?'

'Funnily enough I will actually be in *The Nobody* around that time, *twat, shit*, but it's because I've got a hot date.'

'Oh. OK. Anybody special?'

'Don't know. I joined a dating agency a couple of weeks back and the woman that runs it just called me a few minutes ago and said she'd sorted me out a date. I'm meeting her in there later on.'

'Do you know anybody else who might be able to do it? We're a bit stuck.'

'Leave it to me. I'll tell you what I'll do. I'll have a flick through my record cards and get somebody to meet you there. How's that?'

'Excellent. Thanks, mate.'

Tarquin finished his crisps and left the Café. He was relieved that the meathead wasn't around, everything must have been in order, thank fuck. He was so nearly there now, he'd already made arrangements to pick his fake passport up and the grand he'd just collected would pay for it nicely. The rest of the plan was simple, get the robbery out of the way and steal the part of the cash they were supposed to be giving out to S-Packers. Then he'd simply need to get to the airport, get the first flight to fucking anywhere and start a new life for himself away from all of his troubles.

Shirley had managed to sort everything out nicely in her trip to the village, the tape was safely stored in a deposit box at the bank, all of the necessary papers were signed, all the appropriate funds had been transferred and she'd been and bought a few bits for the boys; some nice new clothes and some toys. She couldn't wait to see their faces later on. She entered the pub through the rear door and called Dave into the kitchen.

'What, Shirley? What's so fucking important that it can't wait. I've got a business to run whilst you're off pissing around.'

Shirley clamped her jaw for a second to prevent her emotions from getting the better of her before saying, 'That's what I want to talk to you about actually, Dave'

'What?' he replied, confused.

'The business.' Her voice quivered slightly.

'What are you going on about, Shirley? And make it quick, there's only me serving.'

'I've sold it.'

The angry permanent scowl that usually dressed Dave's face dropped and was replaced by look of sheer confusion.

'I saw what you did last week on the C.C.T.V. Dave, you're sick.'

His expression didn't change but the colour drained from his face as if she'd opened a valve on the bottom of his chin.

'I'm leaving you, Dave, I'm taking the boys and I'm leaving you. I've taken the money, I've sold the pub and I'm going. Today.'

Dave's brain suddenly caught up with what she was saying and the colour and scowl returned to his face. He pushed her hard into the worktop and grabbed her by the throat. 'And where do you think you're going to fucking go?'

Terrified, Shirley managed to splutter, 'Anywhere!'

Dave tightened his grip and hissed, 'And what makes you think I'm going to let you?'

Shirley concentrated hard, tensed up the muscles in her neck to resist his grip and managed to cough out the words, 'I've secured the tape.'

He let go and Shirley bent over gasping for breath. Dave's tone suddenly changed. 'Y-Y-You've what?'

She looked up at him and smiled. 'It's at the bank in a safety deposit box, and that's where it'll stay so long as you do as I say.'

Dave fell to his knees and began to cry, 'Please don't leave me, Shirley. Please. I'll do anything you want.'

Shirley stood upright and looked down on the broken man who had terrorised her for the last sixteen years. She smiled, she decided she might be able to have a little bit of fun with him whilst she finished off her packing. 'All right,' she said 'you can start by giving everybody free drinks today.'

Maz was definitely inside the club; his car was parked outside. It wasn't the most subtle of motors; a big black

BMW with the registration number CH55 MAZ. There was no mistaking that.

Martin had decided on the perfect solution to his problem, a solution that would get Maz out of everyone's way once and for all. The fact that his car was so easily accessible and recognisable would make everything run that little bit more smoothly.

He pressed the buzzer on the door of the club and waited for a reply. His timing would be key here, he couldn't simply rush this, everything depended on the outcome of this little meeting. He'd have to be careful.

One of Maz's goons answered the door, the big one, the one that Jimbob had described as being the person responsible for smashing his hands and feet to bits and driving him to the hospital. Martin thought the other one was probably in there as well somewhere, the one that had been there the previous Friday. Best to make sure first. No point in there being any nasty surprises.

'Yes,' said Mick. 'Can I help you?'

'I'm Martin, I'm new. I took over from Jimbob last week running the club floor. I need to speak to Maz, it's pretty urgent, there's been a problem.'

'Hang on a minute,' said Mick before closing the door on Martin. He set off upstairs to let Maz know who was at the door. This must have been the lad Maz was waiting for, he hoped he wouldn't have to do any more of his dirty work. What he'd just had to do was enough for one day. He entered the office and said, 'He's here. Said it's urgent and there's been a problem.'

'Fucking right there's been a problem, man, he either lost or sold me fucking pills and coke!'

'I don't think he'd be around here now if he'd sold them, Maz.'

'Who the fuck do you think you're talking to? Just go bring him upstairs, I pay you to do what I fucking tell you to, not to offer your opinion!'

Mick slammed the door closed behind him and furiously made V signs at Maz through it before walking back downstairs and showing Martin through.

Maz was pretty certain that Martin would be coming to explain that the drugs had been stolen, he was too much of a pussy to do anything stupid.

When Martin came through the door he was clearly anxious, Maz couldn't blame him; Martin knew exactly how dangerous he could be. Maz slouched smugly in his chair, pleased at the fear he obviously instilled.

Maz was a mile off the mark as to the reasons for Martin's anxiety. He had no idea as to the seriousness of what was coming his way. As Mick had led him up the stairs, Martin had his eyes peeled the whole way making sure it would be just the three of them in the club.

'What the fuck are you doing here?' asked Maz, 'You're

supposed to be here when everybody else turns up at nine.'

Nine. Martin made a mental note. Everything would have to be done and dusted well before nine o clock.

'Well, there's been a problem Maz. A pretty major one,' replied Martin as Mick took his usual position behind Maz.

Maz had to try hard not to smile, Martin was almost shaking. 'What kind of a problem?'

Martin trembled, his hands in his pockets, this was it. Do it now! 'This kind of fucking problem!' he shouted, pulling out Steve's replica berretta and pointing it straight at Maz.

Fucking hell, thought Mick, *this is all I need. Getting fucking killed by some little nobody.*

Martin shouted again, 'Both of you, backs against the wall. Maz, when you stand up I want you to keep your hands where I can fucking see them or I'll blow a hole in the middle of your face so fucking big you'll look like you just snorted a kilo!'

Maz raised his hands and calmly stood up. 'You're making a fucking big mistake here, kid.'

'Shut the fuck up! And put your back against the wall with your fucking boyfriend now!'

Maz did as he was instructed; anybody stupid enough to pull a gun on him would definitely be stupid enough to pull the trigger. Let him play his game, thought Maz, Martin would get what was coming in the long run.

Martin, with the gun firmly fixed on them, reached into his other pocket with his free hand and pulled out a roll of gaffer tape. He knew it'd be strong enough to hold them, easily, that stuff could hold anything. It was as important to take to a gig as his guitar, it kept mikes and drums in place and kept cables out of the way.

He took a step forward and placed it on the desk in front of them. 'Right Maz, take that tape with one hand, keep the other where I can see it and tie that beef cake's hands together behind his back.'

Maz did as he was told. He removed one thin strip and tied it loosely around Mick's wrists, 'Tighter! And use more of it, go round ten times!' yelled Martin.

Maz sighed and began wrapping the tape tightly around the bouncer's hands as instructed before biting the tape from the roll. Martin shuffled around the side of the desk so it wasn't blocking his view anymore. 'Now do his feet. And don't make me have to ask you to do it more tightly again.'

Mick lay down on the floor and Maz obliged, nice and tightly as he was told. 'OK, now tie your own feet together.'

Maz squatted and wrapped a large amount of the tape around his ankles. He'd tried to be clever by using so much and hoped it would have run out by this time but the stuff just kept on coming, not that it mattered though. Sooner or later Martin would have to drop the gun to tie his hands and then he'd be fucked.

'OK, now kneel down, back to me with your hands behind your back.'

This is it, this is my chance, thought Maz, just before he fell unconscious from the blow to the back of the head Martin had given him with the butt of the gun. Martin tied Maz tightly; he wanted make sure there definitely wouldn't be a way for this fucking worm to wriggle free. As he finished tying Maz up, he could see the bouncer struggling to escape, flapping around on his back like a fish out of water and yelling.

Martin taped up both men's mouths, grabbed his gun and began fumbling around in Maz's desk drawers.

Mick was still struggling on the floor, so Martin took the gun and hit him hard on the back of the head with it, but instead of knocking him out it just seemed to piss him off even more. His wriggling became more frantic. Martin braced himself and hit Mick hard on the back of the head with everything he had. That was it, he was out cold. Martin just had to hope he'd stay that way for long enough to get the job done.

He turned his attention back to the drawers and found Maz's keys. The silly bastard kept them all on one huge key ring, the club, the car, probably his house key too. That would make things easier, but as he lifted them out he saw something else. The fucking bastard! thought Martin as he removed the bag of pills from Maz's drawer. Had he sorted out the burglary himself? If that was the case, Martin had a lot less reason to feel any guilt for what he was doing and the repercussions it would end up having, in fact, he felt even more justified in going ahead with the whole thing.

He grabbed Maz's jacket from the back of his chair, put it on and left the office locking it behind him and headed downstairs, on his way he used his mobile phone to call Tarquin. 'Hi it's me. You know you told me to just play along with it if you were speaking in a camp accent? Yeah, well I'm going Jamaican. And I've got us a car, have you sorted a driver?'

This could possibly be the most ridiculous thing Jerry was ever likely to do in his entire life, but he'd be lying to himself if he denied the perks; getting in the good books at work, having a great story to tell the grandkids and having a good reason to wear a pair of stockings on his head in public were extremely attractive benefits.

He was fumbling around in his secret box searching for

the appropriate pair of stockings or tights to take but he was unsure of robber etiquette. Did he just bring any old tights and let them sort themselves out? Did he cut off the legs or take a stocking for each of them? As he picked out different pairs and inspected them, he realised it would probably make much more sense to have the gusset part of some tights covering the face as it was quite a bit darker than the sheer wave of the legs, that'd definitely offer a lot more protection against identity. That at least narrowed down his choices; stockings and open gussets were obviously out of the question, as were fishnets.

He picked out a few pairs from the remainder and wondered whether or not he should chop the legs off or just have them dangling around the back like a pair of elaborate dreadlocks. He thought that at least, with the latter option, even the tights slipped forward, their faces would be concealed. Some of them were a little older and in a size sixteen, so it could easily happen.

He hoped everybody would appreciate the thought and careful consideration he'd gone to as he bundled them into his pockets.

Martin stood in front of the mirror and looked at himself. He'd loved his long hair and his scraggy shaggy from

Scooby-do goatee beard, but now his face was cleanly shaved and his head housed only a thin layer of stubble. The clippers had taken care of most of it but he'd have to finish it off with the razor just to make sure. There seemed little point in making his face up so he appeared black, the stockings on his head would hopefully be enough to disguise that. He'd just have to make sure he wore gloves the whole time so no witnesses saw his white hands waving a gun around. That would mess everything up, plus since he'd just cleaned it, it would make sure the weapon wouldn't carry a trace of his prints.

CHAPTER TWENTY-EIGHT

FRIDAY 13th July – 4 p.m.

Jerry and Clive were the first to arrive at *The Nobody* and were surprised to receive a beer on the house from Dave. Today was weird in more ways than one. They didn't argue, just took it and quietly adjourned to a table in the corner to enjoy their Dutch courage. Even Paul who was sat with his talking bear at the other end of the pub was sinking a free drink. None of them had the first clue what was going on, and Dave was so preoccupied that he was completely unaware of what was being plotted in his pub whilst he wandered into the kitchen to try and quietly figure a way out of his mess.

'Have you sorted the driver out?' asked Jerry.

'Yeah, Jonny T couldn't do it but he's sending somebody along. They should be here any minute.'

'Who?'

'Dunno, did you get the stockings?'

'Yes,' said Jerry patting his bulging pocket, 'all sorted. Does this driver know what he's doing?'

'I should think so. I can't see Jonny sending me any old idiot.'

'No, you fucking tool! Does he know what we're doing?'

'Oh, Jesus Christ no! I don't want to mess everything up. He'll find out when he's in it too deep.'

'Good.'

Tarquin entered with Martin and took a seat at their table. 'Hi.' said Tarquin, 'This is the guy I was telling you about. Where's the driver?'

Jerry and Clive recognised the bloke he was with but neither of them could put their finger on where from, 'He'll be here any minute. You've got time for a pint, I reckon. They're on the house, if you can find the fucking landlord,' said Jerry.

As they approached the bar they heard the loudest, broadest Rochdale accent they'd ever had the displeasure of listening to. 'Which of you gentlemen is requiring the services of a driver?'

They all turned their heads to glance at Brian. 'Me,' said Clive.

Martin glanced at Brian and his blood began to boil. He couldn't believe this fucking cunt was going to be their driver. He took a deep breath, said nothing and passed the

BMW keys to Tarquin, who promptly threw them at Brian. He caught them perfectly and then glanced into his hands at the keys.

'You need to pick up the car. It's parked at Chameleon in town. Just leave yours there and we'll pick it up on the way back,' said Tarquin.

'No problem. I charge twenty five pounds an hour and my time starts now.'

Brian thought he was pretty shrewd adding five pounds onto his normal hourly rate, but they couldn't help but chuckle at how much it paled into insignificance in comparison to the amount of cash he'd end up transporting.

'Whoa, whoa, whoa!' shouted Brian, running to Clive and Jerry's table and snatching their pints away.

'What?' asked Jerry.

'Drink driving costs lives. We'll have none of that while you're in a car with me.'

'Yeah, but we're not driving mate. You are,' said Clive.

'That's right, young man, I am. My driving, my rules. Barman! Barman!'

Dave popped his head out of the kitchen door and peered into the bar. 'What?'

'Whilst I'm gone, make sure these Yorkshire puddings don't drink anything stronger than orange juice.'

Brian stormed out of the pub and Dave glanced at

Tarquin whilst Martin stood at the bar. 'Look lads. I'm busy. Just help yourselves, will you?'

He couldn't believe he'd just said it but it didn't bother him as much as he thought. He went into the kitchen to ponder once more about how to get out of the mess he was in. He decided he should go upstairs and try to reason with Shirley. Eat some humble pie.

As he got upstairs and looked around the flat it seemed almost unrecognisable, everything was neatly packed away into labelled boxes.

'Almost done,' Shirley said. 'Packed and ready to go. I've spoken to a storage company and they'll pick it all up from here and deliver it as soon as I give them a new address.'

'Don't leave, Shirley. We can work this out I know we can.'

'I don't think so Dave. My children have missed out on half their childhood locked in a cellar, thanks to you and I intend to make sure they don't miss out on anything else.'

'I'll go get them,' said Dave, 'I'll let them out now. We can all go together.'

'You won't go anywhere near them. You've done enough damage, now go look after your precious pub whilst you still can.'

Back downstairs, the plot was underway, 'Right, this is

how it's going to work,' said Martin, 'who's got the stockings?' Jerry raised his hand like an enthusiastic swat pupil in a classroom.

'Good,' said Martin, 'pass them here then.' Jerry handed them over and Martin bundled them into his pockets, 'Thanks, OK, we're going to rob Holme Bridge bank in the village.'

A bank? The others were a lot more nervous now, they had visions of something small, cosy and easy, not a high profile robbery. 'Hang on a minute,' said Jerry, 'this is sounding a bit too risky.'

'Well, you can do the easy bit then,' said Martin.

This sounded a bit more like it. If there was an easy bit to be done Jerry was definitely happy to do it. 'How easy?'

'Really easy. I only need one of you to actually take part in the thing. The rest of you are extras, Tarquin here'll do all the hard work with me.'

'Will I?' asked Tarquin. He wasn't happy about this but as he'd arranged everything, he didn't really have a leg to stand on if he contested Martin.

'Yes, and I've even thought of a way of making your bit easy, too. Don't worry, this is what we'll do. Jerry, you're going to go into the bank first, we're going near closing time, so there shouldn't be too many people in. I want you to join the queue as a regular customer, when you get close to the front, send Tarquin a text message. That's our signal to go, once we storm in I'll take you hostage, that way the bank can't drop any shutters to stop them giving money over, they can't risk the life of a paying customer, you see.'

Jerry intervened. 'So, as far as anybody in the bank's concerned I'm just a normal customer?' he asked, partly pleased but secretly quite disappointed at not getting to wear the stocking on his head.

'Exactly, you're out of the frame.'

'I'm fucking not though!' said Tarquin.

'Yes you are, let me fucking finish. Whilst I'm holding a gun to his head, you're at the front telling them what a maniac I am and that I'm making you do all this. Say what you want, just make sure it sounds convincing and make sure you get her to do it as quickly as possible.'

'OK,' said Tarquin, 'but what about Clive? It looks like he's doing fuck all.'

Martin turned his attention to Clive. 'You told me that the driver isn't going to know what's going on.'

'Yeah,' said Clive nodding.

'Well, you created that problem so you can take care of it. The guy you've managed to choose is a complete cunt of the highest order. It's going to be your responsibility to make sure he stays put. Hopefully, he won't realise what's happening until we get back into the car, but by then it'll be too late. You drop me off at Chameleon then you lot and your spazzy driver can get back into his car and that's the job done.'

'What do we do then?' asked Jerry.

'Not my fucking problem; once you drop me off you lot are on your own. With any luck it'll be me the police are looking for and the other car, you should be long gone. Except you Jerry, you'll still be in the bank. Actually, there is something else you can do whilst you're in there.'

'Oh yeah? What?'

'As soon as we've left, call the police.'

There was some commotion as the group all voiced their concerns simultaneously. 'Let me fucking finish will you?' interrupted Martin, 'Just tell them some Jamaican guy has just robbed the bank, holding you hostage, and you saw them driving away in a black BMW, that'll definitely make it easier for you lot to get away when you've switched cars.'

'Jamaican?' said Jerry.

'You'll see.'

'Isn't calling the police a bit stupid?' asked Clive.

'No, like I've said they'll be looking for that BMW and you'll be in a different car, it only takes a couple of minutes to get from the village to the back of Chameleon. The only person who has to worry about anything is me. You lot will be well on your way, they won't have a clue.'

'I don't like the sound of it. Sounds too risky,' said Clive.

'As long as you don't leave anything behind in the BMW that can link you to the robbery you'll be golden. The only problem you might have is that fucking twat of a driver you've got and I'll deal with him on the way to Chameleon myself, he won't say a peep. I'll leave you lot alone until he gets here. I'm off to go see that guy sat over there for a minute.' Martin pointed over at Paul and his bear and got up off his seat and walked over to him.

'What the fuck is he talking to him for?' asked Jerry.

'Just because he's mentally ill, it doesn't mean he's got no friends, Jerry. Not everybody is as shallow as you,' said Clive.

'Anyway,' said Tarquin, 'who cares, what do you think? Do you think we can pull it off?'

'Sounds all right to me, it all makes sense, the only person implicated is him, and he's pretending to be somebody else. Who the fuck is he anyway? I recognise him from somewhere,' said Jerry.

'Is he in that band?' asked Clive.

'Is he fuck,' said Jerry, 'With hair like that? You've seen them in here they're a right bunch of fucking hippies.'

Tarquin sat quietly smiling. The less they knew the better.

Mick was still sparked out on the floor but Maz had just started to come around. He wriggled around on the floor but there was no way he was getting free, Martin had tied him up too tightly. The concussion and the coke withdrawal were fuelling his anger. He was certain Mick had something to do with this. He wanted to scream but couldn't move properly to remove the tape from his mouth. There had to be a way to break free.

Jonny T had decided to go on the date looking casual. He didn't fancy turning up at *The Nobody* suited and booted. He hoped this date would go better than the last one; that had been a disaster. He'd certainly learned that a meal wasn't a good idea; too much talking required when he had to order from the menu. He hoped the girl would be nicer too; as he thought about his last date his stomach began to turn.

Brian had arrived back at *The Nobody* as fast as the speed limits would allow. The rest of them had got into the car and Martin was urging him to hurry along as it was fast approaching five o'clock and at this rate the bank would be closed by the time they got there. He wasn't having any of it, just kept telling them it was dangerous and drove at thirty the whole way.

The nerves were building for Tarquin. He didn't feel comfortable with his role in the whole thing at all, he just kept thinking that as long as he got out of the country quick enough, none of this would matter. He knew he'd promised Clive that he'd help him dispose of the bodies but it wasn't a promise he'd ever had any intention of following through on. He'd be fine, get his cash, pack it in a case with all of his clothes, get to Europe, buy a scooter, set off somewhere and change his identity again. Disappear without a trace.

Clive was trying to think of something to do or say to keep the driver there if anything happened. The guy made him feel uncomfortable, although Clive did like his taste in clothes. Did he reason with him or scare him? He just hoped he wouldn't have to do anything at all.

Jerry was cool as a cucumber, he had the safe part of the deal, he went in and stayed there. And fucking right too! It hadn't been his fault this time, anyway.

Martin was praying that this car full of absolute misfits

would be able to pull the whole thing off. His life, Jimbob's and the future of the band all depended on this running like clockwork. He felt sick to the pit of his stomach again, like he had all those weeks ago in Blackpool. That had been a laugh though, a joke. This was a million miles away from what he'd got involved with there.

Brian, as he'd been instructed, pulled into Cheapside, a small cobbled street just around the corner from the bank. The village was quiet for the moment but the longer they left it, the more risky it would be, people always seemed to leave work that few minutes earlier on a Friday.

'Here we are,' said Brian, 'safe and sound.'

'OK, lads, I'll go get in the queue, I'll text you when I'm at the front,' said Jerry.

'See you in a bit,' said Martin.

'So, you're collecting some lottery winnings then, are you?' asked Brian.

'Yeah,' said Tarquin. 'He's just off to go check if they've got it ready.'

Jerry left the car and quickly strolled around the corner and into the bank. Martin had been right, it wasn't that busy. He joined the queue and waited as instructed, thinking thank fuck it's not pension day.

Jonny arrived at *The Nobody* and was surprised to see how quiet it was. There were only two people in there, the local loony and he could see the back of a slim brunette girl that, providing her face matched up to the rest of her, he hoped was his date.

Yes. Yes it must be, she was sat drinking what looked like a half of cider with a copy of the *Gazette* on the table in front of her. He didn't go straight over, but waited patiently at the bar to be served.

Bleep, Bleep. 'Right Tarquin, he's ready for us' said Martin. They both left the car and walked around the corner, Martin grabbed Tarquin a pair of tights from his pocket and passed them over. Just as they approached the bank they had a quick glance around, whipped them on and ran straight inside. They were both surprised as they entered the doors at how badly the bank seemed to smell of bollock sweat.

Martin rushed to the front of the queue and grabbed Jerry, who had obviously been stalling, as it looked as if he was fumbling for his cash card. Martin pulled the gun from his inside pocket and pushed it hard against Jerry's face. A little bit too hard for Jerry's liking. In his best Jamaican accent, he shouted, 'OK we want this over with as quickly as you do, so fill up those bags and we'll be on our way. If we have any funny business you'll have this man's death on your conscience.' He tightened his grip around Jerry to make sure he looked genuinely scared as Tarquin produced two carrier bags from his pockets and handed them to the cashier.

'I think she pressed a button!' shouted Tarquin.

'Do you want this man to die? Did you press a button?' yelled Martin.

'No,' sobbed the cashier, 'no please don't hurt him.'

This seemed to hurry her up. 'Please don't piss him off.' Tarquin whispered to the cashier. 'He's fucking crazy. He's told me if I don't do this he'll kill me.'

It took her no more than a couple of minutes to fill the bags. Just the counter drawers though, she never went near the vault. Tarquin wanted Martin to say something to her, make her go back there and fill them even more, but he wasn't about to do that. The quicker they got out of there the better. As the cashier passed the bags to Tarquin, he found it hard to hide the disappointment on his face. There couldn't have been much more than ten grand in the bags. It was barely enough to pay off the lottery money.

Fuck it, thought Tarquin as they fled the bank, he'd just take it, leave them to sort out the mess. As they rounded the corner Clive was relieved that he'd not had to say a word to the driver, he'd just sat patiently waiting for them to return. But as they dived into the back seats shouting, 'Drive!' Brian had a fair idea that something was amiss.

'I will not drive anywhere. You've lied to me,' said Brian.

'We didn't. We've picked up the lottery money, that's all,' said Tarquin.

'And it's standard practice to collect lottery winnings with women's underwear over your heads, is it?'

Jonny was impressed. It was the first time Dave had ever given him a round on the house. Mind you, it was also the first time he'd had to wait around for ages for him to turn up. There was something strange going on, he thought as he walked back to the table. Dave had already asked him to make sure they finished their drinks quickly and left. Not that he minded too much, a pub this quiet with this little atmosphere can't be the most exciting place to romance a lady, he thought.

He approached the table and sat down. 'Hi my name's *fuck, twat, bastard*, Jonny.' Jesus! He'd not even made it through his opening line and he'd fucked it up. It was Dave's fault! Throwing his fucking concentration off like that.

He glanced across at his date and immediately realised it didn't matter, it was just the woman from the video dating place, his date must have dropped out.

'Is there a problem?' asked Jonny.

'No. No problem at all.'

'Well, where's my date?'

'Well, after you came to see me and I was editing your video, I racked my brains trying to think of who I could pair you up with and then it came to me in a flash.'

'And . . .'

'And, I think you're pretty good looking so I thought I'd just keep you all to myself.'

'Fan, *fucking*, tastic!'

Amongst the panic and confusion in the bank, Jerry saw Maz's car go speeding past the front window and, remembering the last part of his instructions, he dialled 999 and asked for the police. 'I'm in the bank and a couple of madmen just robbed us, one had a Jamaican accent and I've just seen them speeding off in a black BMW! He's got a gun!'

It seemed that forcing the gun into Brian's groin was sufficient encouragement for him to get his foot down. Martin and Tarquin removed the tights and threw them on the car floor, Martin also removed Maz's jacket and asked Tarquin to put whatever money they needed in one bag and pass him a bag containing the rest.

'Don't think you've heard the last of this!' yelled Brian. 'I'll tell the police everything!'

'No you won't, Brian,' said Martin, 'Because I know what you did.'

'What? What do you mean?'

Martin leaned forward with his head between the front seats and shouted, 'Think back Brian, you'll remember what I mean! I know your fucking secret! I was there.'

Brian remembered exactly what he meant; he couldn't let this information be leaked out, it would ruin his reputation for certain. 'OK,' he said, 'OK.'

'What secret?' asked Tarquin.

'Don't tell him! Don't say anything!' shouted Brian. 'Or I'll tell the police everything.'

The car screeched to a halt at the back of Chameleon and they all got out, except Martin. He waited until they were away before tucking the gun into his jeans, seizing the bag and grabbing the bunch of keys from the ignition.

He left the car, unlocked the back door of the club and set off towards Maz's office.

Dave had got Jonny, his date and Paul another drink and asked them to kindly sit on the tables outside to finish them off. He closed the door behind them; he couldn't have them seeing where the children had been hidden after all. He was in knots. Shirley would be ready to go any minute and he needed to think of a way to stop her.

He could hear her coming down the stairs and knew she must be ready to go, so he thought fast. He should tell the kids they're going, make it appear as though it was all his idea and then she'd have to take him with her. All she was bothered about was those fucking kids and there's no way she'd want to confuse them or scare them by getting into a shouting match with him in their presence. As he heard her footsteps getting closer, he opened the cellar door.

The boys looked up at him stood at the top of the stairs; he leaned over, rubbing his hands with a wide smile on face and said, 'Hello boys.'

They were panicked. What was he going to do? Last week was evidence enough to them that he was obviously disturbed. They froze in terror as he began descending the stairs.

As Martin entered the office he could see them both struggling to break free on the floor. He was relieved to hear police sirens but knew it didn't give him much time to get done what needed doing. It would be a shame for such a well-constructed plan to fall to pieces now at the last hurdle. He threw the bag of money on the floor and whipped off the tape covering Maz's mouth. Maz started screaming and yelling threats at the top of his voice.

'Right,' said Martin, 'there's your fucking money, but while your hired muscle's tied up on the floor, let's fucking have it. You and me. Man to man.' Martin removed the gun from his belt and slammed it on the table. He knew for certain there was no way a chicken-shit low-life drug-pushing club owner would would fight him man to man when there was a gun on the table.

Martin leaned over to bite the tape around Maz'z hands and as soon as they were free he punched Martin hard in the jaw, knocking him over. Martin was surprised at how hard the punch actually was and couldn't see properly.

Maz frantically removed the tape from his feet and stood over Martin smiling as he kicked him hard in the face. Martin wondered how much more of a beating he would have to take before Maz tried to put him out of his misery.

As Dave reached the bottom of the stairs the boys could see only one option. Run like mad. Instinctively, Billy jumped onto Bobby's back, curled his leg around the front of him and grasped it with his arm which was now over Bobby's shoulder. Back in almost the identical position they were born in, Bobby ran with every inch of strength he had in him, barging past Dave and screaming as he went, out of the cellar, then out of the bar. Shirley took chase behind them, closely followed by Dave.

'You fucking idiot. You fucking think you can do this to me, man? Man to man! Fuck you!' Finally, Maz picked up the gun from the table and pointed it at Martin who was now curled up in a ball on the floor holding his broken ribs.

Maz pulled the trigger. The bang was deafening. Steve had been right, it did sound real. There were two more shots, but these came from a different direction and *were* real. They'd come from the police armed response unit that had just burst through the door. Maz's body fell on top of Martin. He could hear Maz's blood gargling around his throat as he struggled to take his last breaths. He'd taken a bullet to the chest and one to the stomach.

'Thank God you're here,' Martin coughed. 'He's gone fucking mad. He's had us tied up in here all day.' One of the officers lifted Maz's body up off Martin and wiped his bloody face. 'He's been forcing both of us to sell drugs in the club, but we said we wouldn't do it any more.'

He glanced across at the bouncer on the floor and hoped he'd said enough for them to be able to get a story straight when it came to being questioned, and prayed that he'd back him up.

The boys had made it across the other side of the road but Shirley had to stop halfway, gasping for breath. Jonny, his date and Paul were all shocked to see what was happening, but had front row seats from the beer garden.

'Stop!' shouted Shirley.

'Danger!' shouted Brian as he rounded the corner.

Dave had no option, he leapt out into the road and managed to rugby tackle Shirley out of the way of Brian's Corsa, taking the full force of the impact himself. The car hit him in the side and Brian lost control of the vehicle, smashing the car and Dave into a tree.

Clive hadn't been wearing a seatbelt in the back and the force of the crash threw him forwards, buckling the front seat that Tarquin occupied. Tarquin's face smashed into the dashboard breaking his jaw and his nose and, as Clive's body rolled over the seat, he could hear Tarquin's back and ribs snapping and crunching. He heard the windscreen smash as he went through it. Large shards of glass pierced, tore and stuck into his skin as he was flung forward. The force of the crash was so strong that he ended up tangled in the lower branches of the tree.

Brian's seatbelt had saved his life. He sat in shock and silence, but quite the opposite was happening to Paul. As he witnessed the attack from the beer garden, he had a massive moment of clarity, a memory that shone through as clear as day. He was four years old, out with a friend of his and his mother. They were walking from his house to the village and she needed to cross the road to post a letter. 'You two wait here,' she said. 'I'll be back in a second. Theodore will look after you.'

As she was crossing, a Ford Capri came screeching around the corner, its driver concentrating more on swigging the bottle of Jack Daniels he was carrying than watching the road. He hit Paul's mum at what must have been fifty miles an hour.

Paul and Martin saw the whole thing; including seeing Brian back the Capri up and speed away leaving Paul's mum fighting for life on the ground.

That incident had changed Paul from a happy-go-lucky young boy to a man trapped inside his own mind who clung onto a toy bear for security. Now, he fell to the ground as twenty years' worth of memories washed over his brain. Then he glanced at Brian who still sat in shock in the driver's seat of the car. He ran towards the wreckage, pulled the door open, dragged Brian out of the car and began jumping on him, his body, his head and his face. Jonny quickly ran over to try and stop him, but the damage had already been done.

Shirley was frozen in terror as she looked across at the smashed-up mess that used to be her husband crushed between the tree and the bonnet. As she stared at him, his head began to move slowly. He managed to look up at his wife and make eye contact with her but just as he was about to speak, Clive's battered body fell out of the tree smashing Dave's face hard into the car bonnet. Shirley let out a piercing scream but realised there was nothing she could do for him now, but as she glanced up at the small dot in the distance that was her children, she knew she could still make things right for them. She screamed again, this time at the kids to get them to wait and began running after them. They'd managed to get so far away that she didn't know if she'd have the energy to make it.

As they heard her, the boys paused for a moment to take in their surroundings. It was the first time they'd smelled air so clean and fresh. Everything around them looked so beautiful; the trees, plants and grass looked much better in real life. As Shirley caught up and grabbed hold of Bobby's hand, they all heard a siren in the distance and increased their pace. They didn't know where they were going. They didn't even care. They just disappeared into the horizon leaving the wreckage behind them.